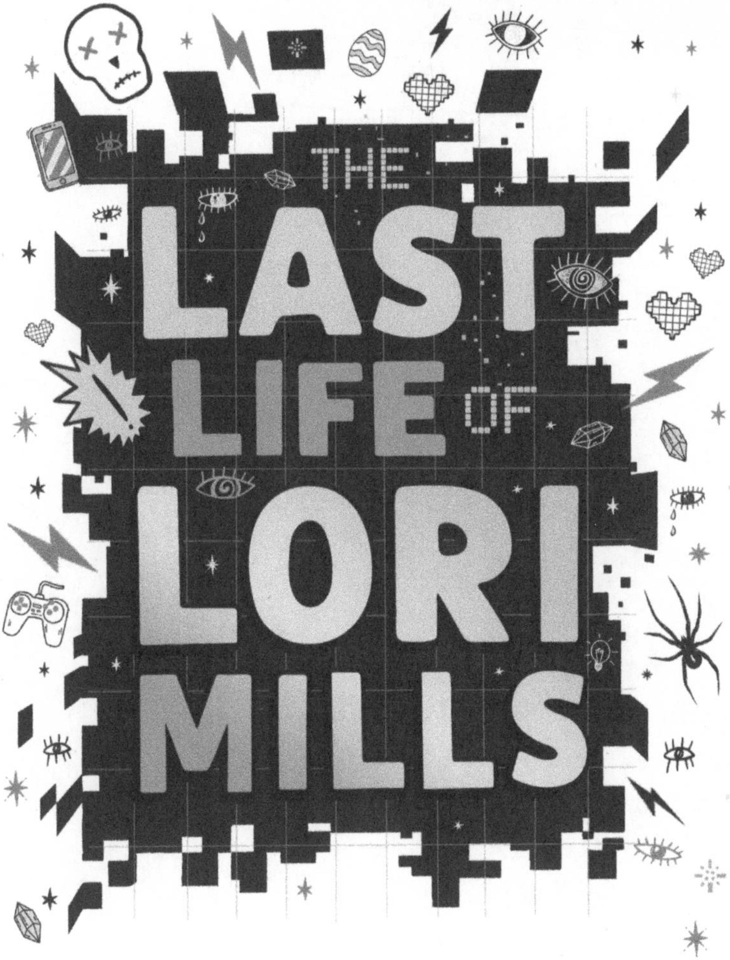

THE LAST LIFE OF LORI MILLS

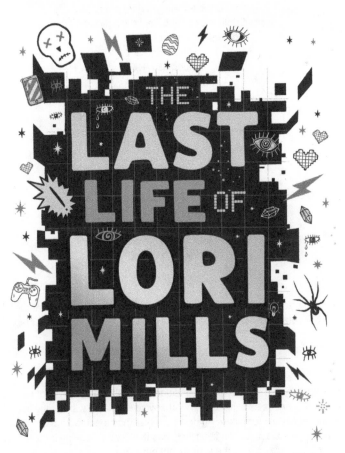

THE LAST LIFE OF LORI MILLS

MAX BOUCHERAT

HarperCollins *Children's Books*

First published in the United Kingdom by
HarperCollins *Children's Books* in 2024
HarperCollins *Children's Books* is a division of
HarperCollins*Publishers* Ltd
1 London Bridge Street
London SE1 9GF

www.harpercollins.co.uk

HarperCollins*Publishers*
Macken House, 39/40 Mayor Street Upper
Dublin 1, D01 C9W8, Ireland

1

ISBN 978-0-00-866648-4

Max Boucherat asserts the moral right to be identified as the author of the work.
A CIP catalogue record for this title is available from the British Library.

Printed and bound in the UK using 100% renewable electricity at CPI Group (UK) Ltd

This book contains FSC™ certified paper and other controlled sources to ensure responsible forest management.

For more information visit: www.harpercollins.co.uk/green

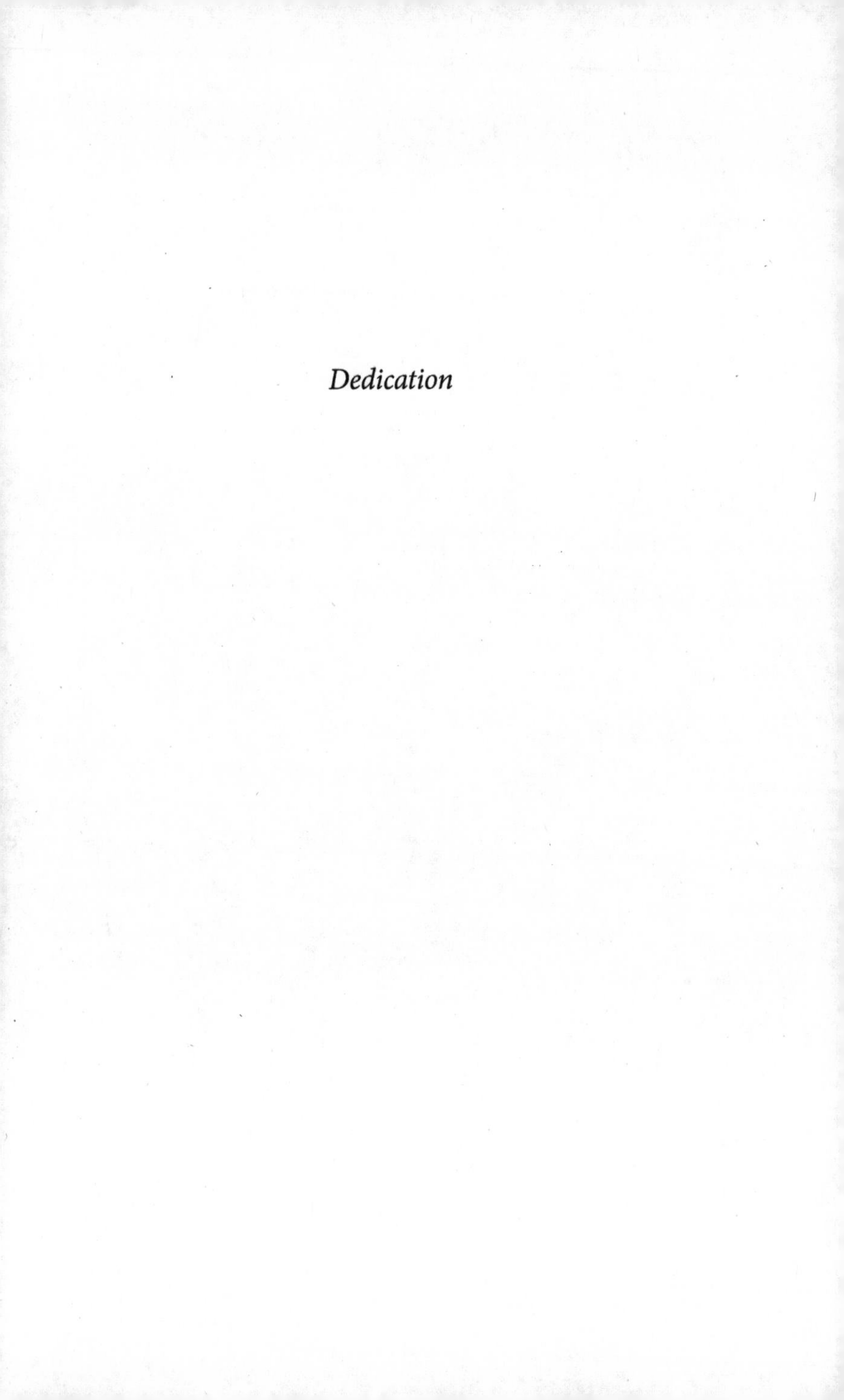

Dedication

<Insert map of upstairs (map 1)>

Artwork to come

<Insert map of downstairs (map 2)

Artwork to come

It's my first night alone and I'm not okay.

Artwork to come

Where Voxminer goes wrong

and I miss you a whole ton

CHAPTER 40

It started around five, when I was having dinner in the kitchen, and Mum was getting ready for work. That's when Jesse the babysitter rang. He was ill.

Mum paced back and forth before the cooker, mobile tight to her ear.

'Could you at least check up on her?' she said. 'Around nine, say?'

There was a pause. I acted like I wasn't listening, but still eating my chicken nuggets. Then Mum sighed and paced even faster. 'Yes, I understand, Jesse. No, no, please don't apologise. It's fine. I'll – I'll find someone else. Get well soon.'

I crossed my fingers under the table and my legs, too, and also my toes. I put my fork down, cleared my throat—

Mum didn't even look at me. 'Not now, Lori,' she snapped.

I scowled at her. 'I didn't say anything!'

'You were going to say something.' Mum scrolled through her contacts. 'I'm not leaving you on your own, and that's that. You're having a babysitter.'

I knew, though, that we were both thinking the exact same

thing: where would she find one at the last second literally humanly possible? Alison-across-the-road is in Spain or something. Plus Mum couldn't even drop me off at Dad's since Dad's on holiday this week with his girlfriend.

I threw on my biggest in-case-of-emergencies pout.

'Muuum, I'll be fine! I'm nearly twelve. Twelve's almost a teenager!'

'"Nearly twelve" is a sneakier way of saying "eleven", Lori Mills.'

'But Charlie's mum lets her stay on her own all the time!'

'Well, unluckily for you, you're not Charlie, and I'm not Charlie's mum.'

But then Mum huffed and folded her arms, and shot the kitchen clock a worried little glance.

I got to my knees on the floor.

'I'll be good,' I said, and I one million per cent meant it. 'I won't make any mess, promise. I'll keep my phone on me all night, and—'

Mum held up a hand and pinched the bridge of her nose. My heart somersaulted. I knew what she was going to say a split second before she said it.

And then she said it.

'Okay. Okay, Lori. Just . . . just this once. Just once.'

She held up one finger to make things as clear as clear could be – and my jaw dropped. I'd convinced her. I'd actually, not-even-joking convinced her.

For the first time ever in my life, I was going to have the house all to myself!

Possibilities exploded in my head like fireworks. I could put the TV on ultra-loud! I could gorge on junk food, set up the Game Galaxy downstairs and play Voxminer all night long!

The fireworks must've shone in my eyes because Mum sat me at the table again and set the ground rules.

1. 'Heaven help you, young lady, if you're not in bed when I get back. I'll be home at half eleven. If I'm any later, I'll text you.'
2. 'What? No! Of course you can't skip your Friday-night bath. Honestly, Lori!'
3. 'No snacks from the cupboard. I will know, Lori. I will know.'
4. 'No. Mess. Or someone isn't getting Big City Kitty for their birthday next month.'
5. 'Yes, I know, I know it's been cold, but don't turn the heating up. Just put on a jumper.'
6. 'You get one hour of Voxminer. Look at me, Lori. Look at me. One. Hour.'
7. 'Keep your phone on you. Keep it on.'
8. 'Oh, for the love of – no, of COURSE you can't go to the corner shop. If the house catches fire – fine, then you can leave. Otherwise, don't leave the house for anything.'
9. 'The TV's off by nine – that's nine, Lori. And the volume stays down.'
10. 'Absolutely do NOT build a blanket fort in the living room. If you want to be treated like "almost-a-teenager", you have got to start acting like one.'

(I tried not to sigh at the last rule. When I'm older, and me and Charlie are famous LumiTube stars and live in a massive house with a giant water park and twenty-seven cats, I'm going to make blanket forts all the time, bigger and blanketier than ever.)

A minute later, with a swift forehead kiss, a warm smile and a stern, 'I love you, and I am trusting you,' Mum left for her shift at Save Shoppers.

The house fell quiet. A streetlamp shone orangely through the glass in the front door.

A thrill shot through my skin.

I was alone.

For the next six-and-a-bit hours,

I.

Was.

On.

My.

Own.

'Oh my goodness,' I whispered. 'Oh my goodness!'

I did a jig by the front door, then turned the heating all the way up and ran upstairs and changed as fast as possible out of my school things. I yanked the duvet, sheets and pillows from my bed and dragged them to the living room.

Once my blanket fort was all set up, I switched off the big light and watched some Monster Kitten Fighting Force on the TV with my stuffed lion, Jonesy. We watched at full volume, with cookies from the snack cupboard and a glass of milk on the carpet. I had my favourite Shimmer Squad novel plus some Detective Mermaid comics. I had my drawing pad with kitten-mermaids on the cover. I had everything a girl on her own could possibly ever need.

Outside, it began to rain. The curtains were shut, but the raindrops smacked hugely against the living-room windows, rat-a-tat-tap: a stormy November night, utterly perfect for curling up in my bright blue Voxminer pyjamas.

Me and Jonesy watched half an hour of VoxFox64, my favourite game streamer, then another episode of Monster Kitten Fighting Force.

And then I messaged Charlie. Using her special nickname, of course, which only I'm allowed to use.

SHOELACE! Guess what??
Guess who has the house
to herself!!!!

Shoelace didn't message back, but that was okay – I already knew about her aunt's birthday party that night. 'Uuurgh!' Shoelace had said earlier in school. 'All my cousins are gonna be there, and they're all boys, too. I wish you could come, Roars.'

(Roars is her special nickname for me, which only she's allowed to use and absolutely no one else on the entire planet of Planet Earth.)

So I put my phone down, then set up the Game Galaxy that Mum got me last Christmas. And, even though Mum's always trying to save money, she didn't buy some dusty, used Game Galaxy 4 with cobwebs and spiders scuttling about in it, but a brand-new, totally unopened Game Galaxy 5.0 Digital Edition!

('Shut up, no way!' Shoelace said when I told her about it on

Boxing Day. But I grinned and told her yes way, and that I couldn't believe it either.)

Then, at last, I lay on my belly in my fort and started Voxminer, aka the Greatest Game in the History of the Universe™©®(etc., etc.).

CHAPTER 39

Voxminer is one of those games where there's no mission you have to complete. There aren't any levels, and there's no main boss at the end you need to defeat. Instead, you make tools and gather resources and things, then use them to build whatever you want.

You can do anything. Make ANYTHING. And, if you don't want to make things, you can just explore instead, and the world goes on forever and ever, for all entire time, and there are forest biomes and mountain biomes, and there are oceans, and islands, and basically every type of rich wild wilderness you could ever even dream of. And it's sooo cool-looking! It's like the anime cartoons that Shoelace always watches, with bright, flat colours and thin black lines around everything.

My favourite thing about Voxminer, though, isn't the graphics, or even all the cool stuff me and Shoelace have ever built together.

My favourite thing of all is collecting Voxfriends.

Voxfriends are these monsters you can catch that help you

do things inside the game. Some, like giga-pup, are big enough to ride, and then you can get round your world super fast. You can even fly on some of them, like ptero-terror, or cirrusaur, which has six wings made from clouds and stardust. Other Voxfriends help you gather resources, while other other ones, like tigget and dodge-dug, help you mine gemstones faster. Some, like whisker-crumb, don't really do all that much, but I love them anyway since they're still super ultra-cute.

So far, I've caught 151 Voxfriends out of the current 457. My favourites I've collected are:

5. **Illumamoth** (you say it ill-LOO-ma-moth). It's a giant moth whose wings light up whenever it gets dark or you go underground.
4. **Squoo**. The cutest, squishiest little squid in the world, which has glow-in-the-dark tentacles.
3. **Dogdecahedron** (dog-decker-HE-dron). It's a dog, but made from pentagons and hexagons. Shoelace reckons it even has a couple of heptagons on it, which is what you call a shape with seven sides! But I've spent ages and ages looking super closely at dogdecahedron, and I've never seen any myself.
2. **Pantherlassa**. A sabretooth panther crossed with a mermaid. It helps you explore the deepest parts of ocean biomes.

Because I'm one of the best swimmers in Year Seven, everyone always thinks my total number-one favourite is either squoo or pantherlassa. But it isn't squoo or pantherlassa. It's:

1. **Blizzuar** (BLIZZ-you-ah). A huge white jaguar that glitters like ice and defends you from wild Voxfriends. It's got two tails made from snow, and it has markings on it that look like snowflakes. It's sooo cute and fearsome! If Mum ever realised how great, amazing and awesome having a cat would be – how amazingly awesome it would be for both of us, even though I'd be the one to feed it every day – blizzuar would 100 per cent be my cat's name.

Not to brag, but two months ago, I managed to catch a blizzuar myself, even though they're one of the rarest ever Voxfriends in the whole of existence. I cornered it at the back of an ice cave. It was SUCH a battle. In Voxminer, you get ten hearts, and each heart is worth four points of health! The blizzuar got me down to my very last heart. But that's when I beat it. And then I literally for real caught it.

I named him Ben.

Shoelace was sooo jealous when I showed her Ben the blizzuar for the first-ever time.

'Where d'you even find it, Roars?' she said. 'Their loyalty score is meant to be off the charts! Trade you all my Voxfriends for it?'

But I didn't trade anything because of course I didn't. Even though me and Shoelace share everything in the wide entire world, Ben was all mine, just for me, and no one else.

CHAPTER 38

Voxminer's main menu appeared on the TV. As it did, I shivered, feeling, for the smallest most whisker-crumb moment in the world, like I was being watched. Like hidden eyes passed over me in the dark or something.

I cuddled Jonesy – the house really was creepy sometimes. But then I shook my head and snuggled up extrally more in my blanket fort and made myself cosier than ever, then selected the world me and Shoelace have been working on after school together.

KITTENTOPIA

The fan in the GG5 whirred.

Then Kittentopia flourished into existence on the TV, and it was bright and wonderful and ours: mine and Shoelace's. Our own private server, just for us, which we started precisely four months and six days ago, exactly one day after finishing primary school.

Kittentopia's got big since then.

BIG big.

It's got a shopping centre for cats and a humongous naughty step for badly behaved kittens. There's a town hall that looks just like the one that appears in all the Big City Kitty games, and there are twin castles shaped like giant cat ears, one for each of our player characters. And, because I insisted, we're also working on a great huge swimming pool deep inside Mount Tuna Paste Mountain, and—

My phone buzzed on the carpet. I jumped! It was only Shoelace, though, FINALLY responding to my message about being alone that night.

No way, shut up!! All to yourself???

I giggled and put down the GG5 controller.

Yes way. House is ALL FOR ROARS
I'm gonna make 2 pizzas
Gonna make a pizza sandwich with cookies in it
MWAHAHAHAHA!!!!!!

Arg jealous!!!
Roars I'm soooooooo boooooooOOoOoOored

Does your aunt have a tablet?
Join me in VM?

Shoelace didn't respond to this. But, I mean, she was at a party and stuff.

I closed the chat and grinned at my phone background, aka me and

Shoelace when it was snowing this April, laughing, Shoelace's black hair and dark skin standing out against the snow. Then I picked up the GG5 controller again, opened up the Voxfriendopedia – a list of every Voxfriend I've caught, along with options of what to do with them – and selected Ben the blizzuar. He appeared beside RoaryCat11 in a puff of icy sparks.

(Side note, but RoaryCat11 is the name of the character I made in Voxminer. The story I invented for her is that she's sixteen and smart and strong and loves swimming and is the best at it. One night, Roary was cursed to turn into a cat. She discovered a potion that stopped her transforming all the way, except it left her with a long black tail and black cat ears that poke from holes in her bright blue beanie. Her skin's pale like mine. Though – unlike me – she doesn't have any freckles. But she wears a black coat and a blue skirt and navy boots and stripy white-and-blue tights, and I swear she is the COOLEST.)

I made RoaryCat11 wander through Kittentopia, Ben following behind like the best Voxfriend in existence – as tall as RoaryCat and as long as my bed. At least, that's how long I think he'd be, if he was in real-life. Then, because it's the first task I always do whenever I open Voxminer, I made them check on all the eggs in the Royal Egg House, aka a cosy greenhouse me and Shoelace spent a whole week building near the end of summer.

I stopped for a second, right outside the greenhouse door. I huddled Jonesy on my lap.

'What d'you think?' I asked him. 'Reckon any eggs have hatched today?'

Jonesy didn't answer. Not that I expected a stuffed lion to answer, of course.

The soft piano music of Voxminer played in my ears. I lowered my voice to a whisper.

'Well, I reckon some might've hatched. Paws crossed, Jonesy!'

Then I marched RoaryCat11 into the greenhouse.

Along with the half-built swimming pool inside Mount Tuna Paste Mountain, and Doctor Skeletail's Litter Tray of Terror, the Royal Egg House is the building I'm most 100 per cent proud of. It's square-shaped and four floors high and made entirely from sparkle-glass. It's surrounded by a moat of aqua-shimmer. The moat is circled by a wall of sunsidian, which shines all night long and scares away wild Voxfriends. When you add all this together, it means the Royal Egg House is the absolute SAFEST building in all Kittentopia.

It's also, by a bazillion miles, the most useful. Because, apart from catching them in the Voxwilds, hatching new Voxfriends from eggs is the best way to collect them. And the quickest way to hatch Voxfriend eggs is by keeping them warm in a greenhouse.

Everyone on the planet who's ever played Voxminer for even one single second makes a greenhouse to keep eggs in.

EVERYONE.

It's like giving your Voxfriends nicknames, or building a secret lair beneath your Voxminer castle. It's what you DO.

The Voxminer sun started setting; the piano music that plays during the day gave way to the lush deep tones that sound at night. I smiled. Then, in the golden twilight, I guided RoaryCat11 and Ben past beds of stomper flowers, under curtains of gravity vines, and down rows and rows of all the Voxfriend eggs me and Shoelace are waiting to hatch – dozens of them, all different shades of blue, pink and red, some with yellow stripes, and some with bright green spots and silver zigzags.

My phone buzzed again.

Sorry, me and cousins playing hide-and-seek

Am typing in wardrobe

Shhh!!!

I messaged Shoelace back at once.

How much longer party?

Literally forever ☒☒

I'm literally turning into a literal skeleton

Here lies Shoelace

Murdered to death by aunt's party

I'll make you a gravestone in VM!!!

Seriously tho when you home?

I waited for another response.

And waited.

Shoelace?

The Voxminer sun had totally set; stars glimmer-twinkled in the Voxminer night. But, in actual real life, wind rattled the living-room windows, and rain lashed against the glass.

I gave Jonesy another squeeze, then checked me and Shoelace's eggs, the greenhouse lit by the twin moons of Voxminer.

None of the eggs looked any different from when I'd checked them before school.

None of them.

I sighed. What a waste of my alone-in-the-house time!

I didn't stick around, however, but made RoaryCat11 run through Kittentopia, down Whisker Street and Scruff-Tail Lane and round the Catnip District, Ben the blizzuar right behind her. Then I made them sneak along a secret tunnel behind the Litter Tray of Terror, and they found themselves in me and Shoelace's half-finished pool inside Mount Tuna Paste Mountain: a massive water-filled cavern shaped like a rectangle, with dark rock walls and a thin path round the edge lit by white moonglow-lanterns.

The pool was quiet since the game music stops whenever you go underground. It was empty. Gloom-flooded.

The sort of place where you might run into something. The sort of place where you might run into—

My phone lit up! It wasn't Shoelace this time, though, but Mum.

Remember, no snacks, no blanket fort, also that's enough Voxminer, it's time to turn it off. Love you

everything. Should still be back at half eleven ☒ xxxx

How did Mum guess I was on Voxminer? Was she watching me through my phone camera?!

I didn't respond, but shot my phone camera a suspicious little glare, then messaged Shoelace.

Roars to Shoelace
Come in, Shoelace!

No answer. And I don't know if it was because of Mum's message, or that Shoelace was still gone, or even because it was stormy and I'd been thinking about creepiness in Voxminer, but, in the cosiness cocoon of my illegal blanket fort, it dawned on me – really, out-of-nowhere dawned on me – how big and empty the house felt when it was dark outside, and when all the lights were switched off.

I quivered. I wondered if I should just follow Mum's ground rules after all and have a bath, then read the latest Shimmer Squad book with Jonesy in bed – since this wasn't the same as Mum just popping to the corner shop for a few minutes. It wasn't the same at all. Mum was at work. Plus my phone said it was only half past seven, meaning she wouldn't be back for hours and hours and—

Ben the blizzuar rubbed himself against RoaryCat11. Little pink hearts appeared in the air around him.

I made RoaryCat11 pat him on the head. 'Good Ben,' I said in real life.

<insert page of eyes>

Artwork to come

My skin chills.

The feeling passes in an instant, but it's an endless instant: a swoop in my blood, a churn in my guts. Like I'm suddenly not alone any more. As though, for one split microsecond, someone is in the room with me, watching me again.

'H-hello?' I call out loud.

No one answers. But hairs still prickle all over – because, on the dark stone wall of me and Shoelace's swimming pool, I finally spot the door.

A door that wasn't there before.

A door I don't remember building.

CHAPTER 37

I sit up straighter, so straight that my head brushes the roof of my blanket fort.

I am sure, I am certain, I am one million per cent certain: the last time I played, that door wasn't there. I would have noticed it. ANY player would notice if their bedroom door randomly appeared in Voxminer.

And it IS my bedroom door.

Not RoaryCat11's bedroom door from her castle in Kittentopia, but a perfect copy of my actual door in actual real life.

Suddenly I wish I hadn't made RoaryCat11 leave the safety of the Royal Egg House. I wish I hadn't led her and Ben down the secret tunnel, into the dark of the swimming pool.

I huddle closer to the TV. My door is pale blue with tons of mermaid stickers and Voxfriend stickers, too, including pantherlassa and illumamoth, and a cute little octopus Voxfriend called porf. That door has some of my best swimming certificates on it. It's got a cool anime drawing Shoelace made for me of Riley from Shimmer Squad. And right in the middle is an ancient sign in felt-tip pen that says

LORI'S LAIR.

Doors in Voxminer don't have porfs on them. They don't have swimming certificates. They don't have felt-tip signs that say **LORI'S LAIR**.wExcept, apparently, this door, rising right in front of RoaryCat11.

I squeeze Jonesy, but keep my eyes on the TV screen, on my bedroom door that should not, should not, absolutely should NOT be there.

'Shoelace,' I whisper, 'did – did you do this?'

When, though? Definitely not this evening, with her aunt's party and stuff. Also, I was working on the pool right before school, when I was meant to be putting my uniform on. Mum caught me. She got really mad! And the door definitely hadn't been there then.

The wind howls.

I stay still for a second. Then I get up, flick on the big light, and sit back down cross-legged in my blanket fort and stare and stare at the TV, thinking, thinking.

A thought prods at me. I pick up my phone and head to voxtures.net.

I'm greeted with a background so violently yellow that it ought to be even illegaler than my blanket fort. In the total yellowness, bright green letters read <website>For All Your Texture Needs!!!!</website>. Underneath that is an ugly grey box, and a message in it says I can upload up to ten different images, though none larger than 4 MB, and JPEGs and PNGs only, thank you kindly.

voxtures.net is . . . not a fancy website. I read once it's done by one person in Japan or something.

Whoever they are, they're some kind of absolute internet wizard, since voxtures.net is a website that lets you upload your very own photos directly into Voxminer. Me and Shoelace used it tons and tons and tons when making the shops on Whisker Street and when we decorated our castles for our player characters. Because, once you've uploaded your photos into Voxminer, you can then put them on to any surface you want. That means any rock or mineral, any floor, ceiling or—

Wall.

I glance at my bedroom door on the TV screen, back to voxtures.net on my phone, then back to the TV. I let out a shaky laugh.

This is how Shoelace did it: she took a picture of my bedroom door, uploaded it to Voxminer using voxtures.net, then placed the photo on the swimming-pool wall. Shoelace is playing a prank on me!

But, even though I know now that it's just a prank, I swallow.

I frown.

'It's a door,' I whisper to myself. 'It's a door, Lori. Why are you so wound up?'

Because something's still off. This doesn't feel . . . Shoelacey. When Shoelace does pranks, they're not weird at all, but just flat-out funny, like the other week with the saucepans, or that time in school with the potato clock.

I message her again.

Oh my god

Shoelace

You're so random sometimes

Relief washes through me when I see that Shoelace is typing. She's back. She's finally back from hide-and-seek.

Thanks I try!!

Wait why am I random lol?

(I roll my eyes. I'm 99 per cent sure Shoelace is the only person under ninety who actually writes lol.)

I found the door you made

Soooo creepy!!!

There's a rain-soaked pause. It's rain with fangs in it, the breed of rain that bites at you: the storm's getting worse.

Then Shoelace replies again and my heart beats faster.

Door?

The door next to the swimming pool

On the wall

Um what you on about Roars?

My bedroom door
You put it there with
voxtures.net right?

WHAT bedroom door???

A growl of thunder; the something-off feeling squirms in my belly. The Shoelace I know would own up instantly. She'd laugh and laugh – lol and lol – then I'd start to lol, too.

I stand up, point my phone at the TV and take a picture to message her.

Then I shriek – because, when the photo appears on the phone screen, I don't see my bedroom door. I don't see Voxminer, or the TV, or even the living room.

<insert eye artwork>

Artwork to come

<insert eye artwork>

Artwork to come

I see eyes.

The eyes are bright blue, bright bright blue – almost white – and they are wide and round and glaring. I see them for just a second, for less than a second, for less than a slice of a SLIVER of a second before I hurl the phone away from me.

Ferocious eyes against the darkness of the screen.

There's hunger in them.

Hunger for ME.

I've found you, Lori, those eyes seem to say.

You are alone and you are mine

and

I

have

come

for

you.

<insert eye artwork>

Artwork to come

It's my first night alone in the house.

I am not okay.

CHAPTER 36

When I pick my phone back up from the carpet, though, the eyes have already vanished from the screen, replaced by a photo of the TV – the very picture I'd expected to see in the first place. And when I glance at the actual TV itself there aren't any eyes there either. All I see is RoaryCat11, the weird copy of my real-life bedroom door, and the shadowy walls of mine and Shoelace's half-finished swimming pool.

I know what I saw, though. I know what I saw on my phone.

I clench a fist.

I know what I saw.

Another rumble of thunder. I grimace, realising that I managed to tread a stray cookie into the carpet and didn't even notice.

Yet I don't even freak out about cleaning it up before Mum gets back. I just brush my foot to get the crumbs off, then close the camera app and message Shoelace.

Get on Voxminer. Now

I know that she can't, that she's at a party and can't just up and vanish to play video games. But she has to. She has to. She has to log on right this actual literal second.

Shoelace I'm serious

Shoelace???????

I shuffle my feet. 'Shoelace,' I hiss at my phone. 'Where flipping are you?!'

Hotness seeps under my skin. I need Shoelace. I need her, need her, need her.

I huff and scowl and chuck my phone on the sofa. Then the hotness-in-my-skin turns instantly cold, since I notice something else on the TV.

'B-Ben?'

When he's not in my Voxfriendopedia, Ben's meant to follow RoaryCat wherever she goes. Blizzuars aren't like ribbit-weasels or snoozefinders – Voxfriends with low loyalty scores, which wander off when you don't pay enough attention to them. No, Ben sticks to RoaryCat like marsh glue, aka the stickiest material in Voxminer. With enough marsh glue, you can even glue fissure-stone to the ceiling of your Voxminer home: that's how sticky it is.

For the first time ever in Voxminer history, Ben's not by RoaryCat's side. He's nowhere even near RoaryCat but aaaages away, down the path that winds round the edge of the pool. Yet, even from a distance, he growls at my bedroom door, his legs tense and his twin tails straight. Exclamation marks flash bright red in the air over his head – the sign that a Voxfriend senses danger nearby.

I stand frozen on the carpet.

Is this a glitch?

Because, if it's not Shoelace playing a prank, that's the only other explanation. The only other one. Absolutely the only other one.

Voxminer's got tons of glitches, mountains of them, actual GALAXIES of them. Me and Shoelace always watch them together on LumiTube. My favourite is the VoxHead glitch, where your player character's head gets replaced with a random Voxfriend's, plus I also love the one that lets you dash at 111 times your normal speed, aka the 'one-one-one run hack'.

What kind of glitch, though, knows what your bedroom door looks like?

Also, what about the eyes? The eyes on my phone?

Slowly, I pick up Jonesy, then sneak past my blanket fort to the living-room door. Because a dark thought, the worst thought I've ever, ever had, is galumphing through my head.

There is another explanation. A third one. A secret one.

I have been trying very, very hard not to think about the secret third explanation.

Now, though, with the storm picking up and Ben the blizzuar growling on the TV, a hundred LumiTube videos flood through my mind, with titles like 'Surviving the 666.exe seed in Voxminer', and 'Did I see HER in Voxminer?? (Scary)', and 'Top 15 HAUNTED Voxminer Creepypastas That Will Make You Ugly Cry (SG VoxThing Error 548 Aggie Wants To Play)'. Me and Shoelace always watch them when we have a sleepover. They're sooo freaky! And that's not even mentioning the VoxFox64 streams where he goes hunting for ghosts and stuff. Or, if not ghosts, then he's searching for the dreaded Cassette Head. Or Entity 11-18-11. Or The Maestro in the Deep.

'Teenagers aren't scared of doors,' I tell myself. 'They're not scared of dumb, stupid doors in dumb, stupid Voxminer.'

With a last glance at dumb, stupid Voxminer, I clutch Jonesy tighter, then open the living-room door and rush into the downstairs hallway and turn on the light and race to the kitchen. I switch on the radio and turn the volume all the way up. I never use the radio, but I can still find the channel Cheeky Days FM since Mum listens to it all the time. Right now, there's a group on called B'Dazzled, who are one of Mum's favourites from a gazillion years ago.

The rain gets even louder, so loud that I hear it over the radio. I feel all chilly, even though the heating's on as high as it goes.

Then I realise my phone's still on the sofa in the living room – but I'm not going back for it. There's no WAY I'm going back in there. Not until Mum's home from work.

The kitchen clock says it's exactly one minute to eight.

I swallow.

'I can do it,' I whisper. 'You can do it, Lori. You can last three and a half hours. Um, three and a half hours and one minute.'

With that, I hurry upstairs and switch on the landing light, the bathroom light and Mum's light, too, and I play the prehistoric CD player in Mum's room as loud as it goes. There's already a CD inside. It's an album by Avenue Ladz, who are another of Mum's favourite old bands. Between that and the kitchen radio, the house comes alive with music.

I march to my bedroom and yank the door open and step inside, then slam it behind me and jam the handle with my desk chair.

I can deal with this. I'm just two weeks from twelve, and twelve's almost nearly a teenager, which means I can deal with this.

CHAPTER
35

I hug Jonesy, press myself against my bedroom wall, and stay as still and silent as a snoozefinder. Then I hug myself and twirl my hair a bit with my finger. (I'm always telling Mum that I'm old enough to cut my hair how I want, and that I don't want long hair any more, and that short hair is way cooler-looking, plus better for swimming! Yet somehow, when I'm actually in the hairdressing seat, I can never quite go through with it.)

A few minutes more pass, and then I start feeling normal again. Normal-ish. In the region of normal.

For one thing, thanks to the evil radiator under my window – which is faulty and impossible to ever turn off, ever – my room is always sooo much warmer than the rest of the house. Shoelace named the radiator helioserpent (HE-lee-oh-SIR-pent), after a Voxfriend you always find slithering about in lava lakes in volcano biomes. Usually, I HATE how hot helioserpent makes my room feel. But, right now, I'm kind of thankful because the heat is actually super nice. It's nice. It's nice to be warm in my snug little bedroom.

Also, although my sheets, pillows and duvet are imprisoned in the living room, at least my mattress is new and squashy. Plus I have a great massive cushion shaped like a dolphin, and I have tons of stuffed animals, too, mostly sea critters.

Me and Shoelace call them the Sea Gang. They're my friends.

I pile the Sea Gang into a fluffy mound, but I don't lie down yet, since part of me wants to open my laptop and search online for Voxminer glitches. Except what if I can't find the answer I want? Or what if I do, and the answer's horrible? What if I'm being haunted by Sh—

(Stop that! my mind snipes at me. She's not real, dummy. She's not even real.)

So I gulp, and rather than open my laptop I pick out my second favourite Shimmer Squad novel from my bookshelf – Wrath of the Deep – then curl up on my duvet-less bed with the Sea Gang.

Shimmer Squad is the best. Series. Ever.

Five classmates in high-school detention get magic warrior powers, then have to figure out how to get along while defending Earth from an invasion from an evil dimension. There's Tabatha, Ariadne, Riley, Jacob and one whose name is Natalie, except everyone calls her Night Shade. Night Shade is most people's favourite. But my favourite of all is Riley, because of her awesome water powers.

Team Shimmer Squad are smart and cool, and so grown-up, and scared of nothing.

They're definitely not scared of doors.

They are definitely, definitely not scared of doors in Voxminer.

It's only when I reach chapter six that a flash of lightning lights up my window and makes me jump. I should've shut the curtains! But then I notice my Monster Kitten alarm clock says it's already past nine, and I forget about the curtains at once. Over an hour has slipped by. And, now that my head's clearer, I start remembering more and more Voxminer glitches, so many that my cheeks go hot – not from fear, or from helioserpent, but because of how silly I suddenly feel.

Thunder wraps round my bones, rattles them, clattles them.

I think of the infinite aqua-shimmer hack. Of the bewitched-Voxfriend glitch, and of an ultra-cool-yet-hard-to-pull-off glitch that VoxFox64 calls death clipping.

My bedroom door in Voxminer was a glitch.

It must have been. It MUST. I don't know how it happened – I can't BEGIN to think how it happened. Yet it's the only thing that remotely makes 100 per cent sense.

And did I really see the eyes on my phone?

Wind batters my bedroom window. There's not much to see through the glass – just the backs of the houses opposite the garden, and they're all bathed in that murky purple-brown glow you only see at night, and only when it's cloudy. (I never used to see the glow before moving to the city. I think it's from all the streetlamps reflecting off the clouds? All the billions of houses with their lights still on?)

The rain smacks so heavily against the glass that it's like I'm staring out from an underwater Voxminer base. Yet the storm isn't enough to make me forget the eyes, those bright blue eyes that glared at me from my phone screen.

'I can't have seen them,' I whisper, and I frown and think things through in my head.

The living room was dark. I'd been tense and already ultra-creeped-out, and I saw the eyes for only the absolute smallest second in the known universe. Am I certain, actually utterly certain, about what I saw?

I give Jonesy another squeeze – then gasp because, oh my goodness, what am I doing? What am I even doing, just lying in my room being freaked out by a glitch in a video game?! What's Mum going to say when she gets home and sees that:

1. I'm not in bed. Heaven help me, etc., etc.
2. I haven't even run my Friday-night bath, let alone actually had it.
3. The snack cupboard is a mess.
4. The whole living room is a mess.
5. The heating's all the way up.
6. I've blatantly been playing Voxminer for at least a million hours.
7. I don't have my phone on me.
8. I haven't left the house, so that's at least one thing I'm doing right. But it doesn't even matter since Mum's probably going to banish me anyway.
9. It's past nine and the TV's still on.
10. Also, there's a blanket fort in the living room.

    10a. A big blanket fort.

    10b. A BIG blanket fort.

    10c. Did I mention the blanket fort yet?

The blanket fort Mum specifically said
NOT to build?

I count them on my fingers: that's nine broken ground rules out of ten. And that's without even mentioning the radio pounding in the kitchen and Avenue Ladz still blasting from Mum's room, since the CD player's on repeat.

I shoot Jonesy a weak smile. 'What do you say?' I ask him. 'Should we clean up?'

He stares back with his worn button eyes. I take that as a yes.

So, shoving Voxminer from my head as best I can, I get up, unwedge the chair from my door handle and hurry downstairs to the living room. Slowly – with a deep breath, and reminding myself that almost-nearly-teenagers aren't scared of video games – I switch on the big light.

Everything is as I'd left it.

In a STATE.

It's like when you blow up a house in Voxminer with crystal-dynamite! My blanket fort takes up half the room, cookies are still trodden into the carpet and my phone is on the sofa. Everything is 100 per cent precisely, exactly the same.

Everything except Voxminer.

The Game Galaxy 5 should've gone to sleep forever ago. But it hasn't. Voxminer is still on the TV. It's still on the TV, and the swimming pool has changed again.

There's no one else in the house. No one except me and Jonesy and the Sea Gang.

Yet, despite the fact that no one else is in the house, despite the fact that Shoelace can't play at the moment, and despite the fact that me and Shoelace are the only ones in the galaxy who know the password to Kittentopia, two new lanterns have appeared on the screen, one either side of my bedroom door, each of them freakishly blue.

Like eyes.

I think I hear a whisper, too. Or maybe it's the rain, or my imagination flying into hyperdrive. Real or not, though, the whisper says:

LORI...

LORI...

LORI.

CHAPTER 34

Cheeky Days FM and Avenue Ladz both still sound in my ears. It makes me feel the teensiest smidge braver.

I dig my nails into my skin.

'Hello?' I breathe into the living room.

No one answers. And, apart from the music, there's nothing but rain and thunder and rattling windows – which probably means I really did imagine the whisper, right?

Even so, I shut the living-room door with a click so that nothing can sneak up on us.

Then I fix my eyes on the TV screen.

On my bedroom door on the swimming-pool wall.

On the two blue lanterns that look so much like eyes.

Ben the blizzuar's not growling any more. He's crouching low, twin tails between his legs, and the exclamation marks over his head have been replaced with wide-eyed purple emojis.

Fear symbols.

Fear symbols only appear above Voxfriends with low boldness scores. I've never seen them over Ben before.

Never.

Never.

'Shoelace,' I whisper. I snatch up my phone from where I chucked it on the sofa. Its weight feels good in my hand. 'I swear to God, you'd better be home by now.'

But though I message her again, then again and again and again, Shoelace doesn't answer.

I swallow, then do something I almost never, ever do: find Mum in my contacts and dial.

Her phone rings.

Pick up! I think wildly. *Pick up! Pick up!*

Her phone keeps ringing. It rings and it rings and it rings.

Then the ringing stops, and the answer-machine lady says, 'I'm sorry, but the person you have called is not available. Please leave a message after the tone.'

I groan. End the call. Try again.

'I'm sorry, but the person you have called is not available.'

I try one more time.

'I'm sorry, but the person you have called—'

Why isn't Mum picking up? Isn't she meant to have her phone on her for emergencies?!

'Where are you?' I hiss. This time, I don't hang up on the answer-machine lady, but wait for the tone, then leave a message.

'H-hey, Mum! Hi, um . . . hi. I'm okay. Can you call back? I love you. Sorry. I'm fine. Call me back. I love you.'

I grimace and hang up – and should I call Shoelace, too? Would that be weird? Usually, we just message each other or speak online through Voxchat. I've never actually, you know, called her. Like, on a phone.

Even so, I find her in my contacts, swallow, then dial.

Her phone doesn't even ring, but goes straight to the answer-machine lady.

'I'm sorry, but Crazy Charlie Ruler of Penguins is not available. Please leave a message after the tone.'

Despite everything, I let out a snort. I remember when Shoelace recorded that. Oh my goodness, it must have been almost a whole entire year ago!

I hang up, shove my phone in my pyjama pocket, then stare at Ben cowering on the TV.

At my-bedroom-door-that-shouldn't-be-there.

At the two blue moonglow-lanterns that glare straight back at me.

Another gust slams against the living-room windows.

I clench my fists.

I can't TAKE it any more.

So I say what I should've said the instant I saw that mysterious door in the first place. 'That's it,' I snap at the TV. 'I'm SWITCHING YOU OFF.'

As though in response, I hear the whisper again. This time, I know it's not my imagination. It's louder, clearer and it's 100 per cent definitely not the wind: because it comes from the TV speakers.

It's the door.

My bedroom door is speaking to me.

I stare at it in totally total horror.

LORI,

it coos.

IT'S TIME TO OPEN ME, LORI.

CHAPTER 33

The door speaks slowly. It draws out my name, and, though it's a little louder than before, it's still so quiet that I can't tell if it's got a grown-up's voice, a boy's voice or a girl's.

But I'm not sticking around to find out. I stride past the blanket fort, place Jonesy on the carpet, then kneel down and switch off the GG5.

Nothing happens.

Or not nothing exactly. Ben the blizzuar turns and faces me through the screen – as in actual real-life me kneeling on the living-room carpet.

I gawp at him.

Ben crouches low, folds his ears against the back of his head, and his glittering twin tails stand on end. The snowflake markings on his fur turn deep purple. Ice spreads across the tiles round each of his four paws. He's in his attack position.

And then he growls at me. Really superly growls at me.

I shriek. It's a sound I've never heard from him before, a noise I don't reckon ANY Voxminer player has heard. Four hundred and fifty-seven Voxfriends to collect, yet there are only a handful of sound effects between the absolute entire lot of them.

Ben's growl is NOT one of those sound effects. It sounds . . . real. There's fear in it. A warning in it. He's warning me to stay back, stay well-the-heck back from the TV.

I hit the GG5 off again, smash the power button, whack it as hard as I can.

Voxminer still doesn't switch off.

LORI,

the door whispers. Somehow, its voice cuts through the wind, the rain, the pop music blaring through the empty house, and the noise of Ben's growling.

LORI.

'SHUT IT!' I yell. I jump up and reach behind the TV and rip out the plugs, all of them.

Voxminer still doesn't turn off.

The TV does not. Turn. Off.

My face burns, my heart pounds, and I step back sharply as though the TV's grown fangs or something.

OPEN ME, LORI,

says the door.

YOU CAN SEE ME. HEAR ME. THAT MEANS YOU'VE ALREADY PROVED YOURSELF MORE SUITED THAN MOST. ENTER ME AND SEE HOW DEEP THE EGG NEST GOES.

There's a thought in my mind, a thought I've tried to bury as hard as I possibly can. But now it grows so strong that it blasts free and tears loose in my head, and there's nothing I can do to stop it.

And the thought is this.

It's fun pretending Voxminer is full of ghosts. It's fun to pretend that, if only you search hard enough, you really will come across the demonic VoxThing in the deepest deeps of the deepest caves. It's fun pretending that if you explore the furthest reaches of your world on the night of the thirteenth, and if you type into Voxchat 'I'm happy I'm ready I'm happy I'm ready I'm happy I'm ready', then Absence.8548 will find you, and he'll make your game crash, and corrupt all your save files.

HOWEVER.

It's even more fun pretending that Voxminer isn't packed with ghosts at all, but that it's haunted by just one particular ghost, who me and Shoelace have spent sooo many nights searching for, and who tons of people swear they've seen.

Shade Girl.

If you know about Voxminer – if you've ever even just heard

of Voxminer – you know all about Shade Girl. She looks like any other player character you'd see in the game, except she's made completely from shadow and her eyes are two glowing dots of freakish blue.

Some say she was a real-life girl once, but she was murdered one night and her spirit entered the game, and now she's trapped there forever. Others say that Wolf and Tiger Studios, the people who made Voxminer, summoned a demon. But then the demon was too powerful, so Voxminer is secretly a great huge prison made just to contain it.

Either way, they say Shade Girl only appears when you're playing by yourself, and only at night. They say she watches you from far away. They say that, if you spot her, you only see her for a split-split second before she vanishes into nothing.

Then the weirdness starts. Your favourite buildings disappear. Everything in your inventory turns into swamp gunk, aka the most useless material in the universe.

Those are the nicer stories. Some reckon she sucks you into Voxminer and devours your soul and turns you into an undead Voxfriend, or worse.

My breath quickens.

Am . . . am I being haunted by Shade Girl?

But for real?!

Whack. In my hurry to get away from the TV, I kick over my milk from earlier and send it flying over my Detective Mermaid comics.

Whumph. I tumble into the blanket fort. Sheets and pillows collapse on the floor.

My knee stings; I suck in a breath; I yank up the left leg of my pyjama bottoms and rub my skin in a tight little circle.

'I'm dreaming,' I hiss through gritted teeth. 'I'm dreaming.'

Because did my bedroom door really say what I think it said? Egg nest? What's it blabbering about eggs for? I can't, I can't have heard it right. It MUST have said something else, or I'm really, honestly just dreaming, dreaming, dreaming.

Yet my knee still stings, and I press my fingers harder against my skin, and I can feel my bones underneath. The air boils from the heat being on full blast all evening, and lukewarm milk soaks miserably into my pyjamas and mixes with cookie crumbs on the floor. The storm batters the windows. It assaults my ears. Ben growls again, and ancient pop music still blares through the house.

I am not dreaming this.

I am awake.

I'm sitting on the floor, and my forehead suddenly pounds, and I am hideously, one trillion per cent AWAKE.

I grab Jonesy and stuff him in my pyjama top so that his head pokes out from my collar. I know it sounds weird, but I like his lion softness against my chest. I like knowing he's there and that I have a friend with me. If only I had Shoelace here, too.

'What do we do?' I whisper to him.

That's when the kitchen radio and Mum's CD player stop playing.

At the same exact time.

CHAPTER 32

A few weeks ago, me and Shoelace's English teacher, Ms Harris, told the class that if you come across a tiger in the wild, most people's instinct isn't to run but to keep as still and quiet as totally, humanly possible.

Shoelace put her hand up. 'Don't you mean keep as quiet as a snoozefinder, Ms?'

The class giggled. Ms Harris just stared at her. I'm roughly eiiighty-five per cent sure she didn't know what a snoozefinder was.

But then I remember glancing at Shoelace, and Shoelace shrugging back at me, and I know she was thinking the exact same as me: why wouldn't you run from a kid-eating tiger? Why would you stand there?

But I get it now. It's not something I can put into words, but I get it. Because the instant the music stops every muscle in my body screeches at me not to move.

If I'm still, maybe I'm not as obvious.

If I'm quiet, maybe I won't be spotted.

Spotted by what, I've got nooo idea. But something bad.

Something D-for-absolutely-Dreadful.

I keep my eyes on the screen and wait for my bedroom door to whisper again. All I hear, though, is the screaming wind and thunderous rain. It's like the door's trying to trick me into thinking it never said anything at all.

Which leaves the question:

Should I actually for real open it?

I shiver. Of course I shouldn't. What a 100 per cent stupid question! What I need to do is run upstairs and lock myself in my room until Mum gets back.

Except what if that's what the door secretly wants? What if Shade Girl's somehow crept out from the game into real life, and she's already waiting for me upstairs? What if that's why the music stopped? What if Shade Girl turned it off?

My eyes water but I'm not going to cry. I'm two weeks from twelve, and twelve years old is almost a teenager. So I am not, I am not, I am NOT going to cry.

(Except Team Shimmer Squad don't have any trouble crying, says the tiniest tiny thought in my fear-frazzled mind. Riley cries all the time, and she's the coolest one of all!)

I sniffle and clutch Jonesy – and, suddenly, I wonder if the best thing to do is face things head-on, like how Team Shimmer Squad would handle this.

Like how Shoelace would handle this.

Shoelace wouldn't even think about it. She'd just rush in and do whatever it is she'd end up doing.

My fingers tremble.

Then I pick up the GG5 controller (it's wet with milk, though none got on any of the buttons, thank goodness), and I wipe it on the collapsed blanket fort, tilt the joystick forward and make RoaryCat11 creep towards my bedroom door. This time, Ben the blizzuar follows her, snowy tails on end and ears alert.

'It's okay,' I whisper to him. I don't know if he can hear me, but it feels like the right thing to do. 'I swear it's okay. Swear on my heart.'

I imagine Shoelace cross-legged next to me, comforting Ben as well and egging me on.

Then I lift one hand off the GG5 controller . . . I scrunch my fingers in the air like I'm giving imaginary-Shoelace's hand a pretend little squeeze . . .

Before I can change my mind,
I open the door in Voxminer

and march

on

through.

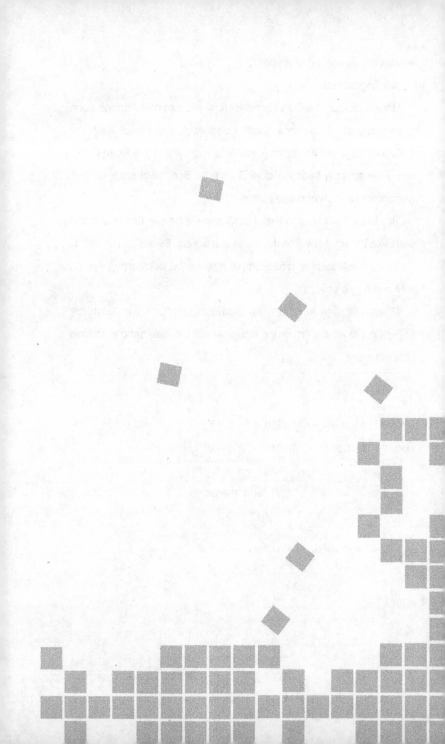

Artwork to come

Where I wish we were hunting ghosts together

CHAPTER 31

A crash of thunder. The wind groans; the rain picks up; the windows rattle. The big light flickers in the living room.

I yelp. But the flicker lasts only an instant, so I gulp and stay right put, right where I am on the carpet, staring at the TV.

My heart trips over itself.

To be honest, I don't know what I was expecting to find when I opened the door. A Voxminer version of my bedroom, but some weirdo nightmare version of it complete with monsters and undead Voxfriends? Something else? A cave? An evil temple? Pure complete darkness, like you find when you use death clipping to enter the Blockless Abyss?

It's not my bedroom, though, that greets RoaryCat11, or a cave or a temple or even plain old blackness, but an empty corridor, and the corridor is long and thin, and it's got a low, low ceiling. All the surfaces are covered in little white tiles, like the changing rooms in me and Shoelace's local swimming pool (the real swimming pool, I mean, not our pool in Voxminer), and the whole corridor is brightly lit with white moonglow-lanterns built into the ceiling. My swimming certificates line the walls, except there are a million of them instead of the twenty-six that exist in real life. It means I see my name over, over, over and over:

Lori M., 25 METRES

Lori M., 100 METRES

Lori M., 500 METRES

Lori M., 1,000 METRES

Lori

Lori

Lori

Lori

I make RoaryCat and Ben creep down the corridor; every few seconds, I spin RoaryCat round to glance back at my bedroom door. I keep betting the door's going to close by itself, but it never does. It stays wide open, taunting me, teasing me by doing nothing at all.

'I've got my eye on you,' I hiss at it. Really, though, I mainly say it since the wind-rain-rattling is getting unbearable.

Except that's when it dawns on me that outside the rain has stopped.

Hairs prickle on my neck. It was pouring, but now it's stopped, and I couldn't even tell you when it stopped. Even the wind has suddenly become almost-all-the-way quieter.

I curl up smaller on the ruins of my blanket fort. It's weird, since I would've reckoned that the storm going away would make things less creepy, not more creepy. Yet it's the total opposite. Like the night is holding its breath.

Like it knows something I don't.

RoaryCat and Ben hurry down the silent corridor for what I swear is miles. The whole time, swimming certificates neatly line the walls on both their left and right.

Lori

Lori

Lori

Lori

The tiles begin to change. They're no longer small and white, but large and cream-coloured, and the ones on the floor turn sickly green. They look almost like the tiles from my old swimming pool, from ages and ages ago, from before Dad left, and me and Mum moved to the city . . .

I should be recording this.

Not on my phone. The thought of opening my phone app again makes me shiver-cold all over, makes me feel properly shaky on the carpet. But I can use the screenshot button on the GG5 controller, since holding it down lets you record clips of up to thirty seconds.

Or rather, holding it down used to let you do that – because, when I try recording the corridor, a message appears on the screen that says: **FUNCTION NOT AVAILABLE.**

'Seriously?' I hiss. 'Are you kidding me?'

I try again. **FUNCTION NOT AVAILABLE.**

I try taking some normal screenshots instead. **FUNCTION NOT AVAILABLE. FUNCTION NOT AVAILABLE.**

I hear a buzzing sound.

It creeps from nowhere, low and electric, and it makes me totally forget about videos and screenshots. There's something familiar about it. I can't put a finger on what.

Then I realise the buzz gets louder whenever RoaryCat walks under the moonglow-lanterns, and I gasp: it's the same noise that some of the lights at my old primary school used to make, the big long fluorescent-tube ones in the corridors outside the classrooms! I remember our Year Six teacher, Ms Newt, saying those lights irritated her, and that she wished the school would finally get rid of them.

Moonglow-lanterns are not supposed to sound like fluorescent lights. They're not meant to sound like anything. They're meant to be quiet.

Fluorescent-light-buzz is the noise of parents' evenings, or when you have to stay behind after hometime. I'm odd, I guess. I like the buzz of fluorescent lights. In fact, secretly, I love-in-general being in school after hometime – and I especially loved being in primary school after hometime.

St Peter's was super old, from Victorian times, or at least the

Juniors' building was. I miss the oldness. There was an ancient theatre stage in the hall, a dank basement and big draughty classrooms, one each for Year Three to Year Six; upstairs, there was a long cold corridor, with the doors to the Year Five classrooms on one side, and the doors to the Year Six ones on the other. It was all sooo creepy! Yet it was the fun kind of creepy where you weren't in any real danger, since there were still teachers nearby in case you needed them.

Whenever you stayed behind after school in St Peter's, half the lights were switched off. But the fluorescent lights were always still on for some reason, alllwaaays, and you could hear them buzzing from a mile off. Zzzzz.

Last Christmas, me, Shoelace, and whoever else had an acting part had to stay back for extrally-extra-and-especially-special after school nativity rehearsal. There was a moment when the two of us got sent from the hall and upstairs to our classroom because Ms Newt had accidently left her script on her desk, aka the copy with all her notes on it.

Me and Shoelace were shepherds – we had on these white cape-things that made us look like ghosts – and we were alone. The Years Five and Six corridor was brightly dark. That's what I call that only-in-winter kind of dark when everything's really lit up, yet it still feels dark since the windows are black, and the shadows are colder and heavier than normal.

It was quiet. Quiet, that is, apart from the buzzing fluorescent lights.

Shoelace nudged me and made me jump.

'Roars! Wanna look for Fireplace Dave?'

I giggled. Fireplace Dave was one of those stories that everyone in St Peter's knew, but mostly we acted as though it was just a joke. Except deep down, deep, deep down, you'd catch yourself wondering if maybe it wasn't a joke after all. You'd think about how old the school was, and how, back in Victorian times, kids used to have to sweep the chimneys as a punishment (or that's what Shoelace reckoned at least). You'd think, too, about children getting wedged and stuck in the sooty blackness, then burned alive by lazy grown-ups who'd forget they were up there.

The school chimneys hadn't been used in a long, looong time.

What would you find if you looked inside them?

Who would you find?

I raised my hands and wiggled my fingers in the buzzing corridor.

'ShoooOOOoooeeeLAAAcccceeee!' I said in a ghost voice. 'It's meeeeee, Fireplace DAAAAAAaave! I'm coming to GET yoooooouuuuuu!'

Shoelace grinned. In a ghost voice of her own, she said, 'But you CAN'T get me, Fireplace Dave. For I am the ghooooOOOooost of the chiiillllllMMMMney, and I'm coming to get YOOOOUUUU INSTEEEAAAaaaad!'

I shrieked with laughter. Shoelace laughed, too, and chased me down the corridor.

But, before we reached the Year Six rooms, the fluorescent lights got suddenly brighter, and their buzzing grew louder, ULTRA loud.

zzz-zzz-zzz-ZZZ

We skidded to a stop. Gawked at the lights.

They got brighter, BRIGHTER, **BRIGHTER.**

Then–

POP.

With a last blinding flash, they went out. The corridor was plunged into 100 per cent blackness.

We SCREAMED. But thank God Shoelace had her phone on her because she whipped it out, flicked on the torch, and I grabbed her hand and we absolutely LEGGED it – we legged it all the way back to the hall!

Everything was in chaos, there. It turned out there'd been a power surge and then a blackout, which meant the lights were off through the whole entire school. Ms Newt was so busy trying to calm twenty screaming children that she didn't even ask us about her script.

But though me and Shoelace both knew, now, that the lights-going-out had nothing to do with Fireplace Dave – not really – we never forgot that feeling of running for our actual lives from what we thought was a bloodthirsty ghost. We never forgot the absolute THRILL.

We wanted more of it.

More.

We spent the whole rest of St Peter's totally obsessed with the cold, buzzing, brightly dark corridor right outside our Year Six classroom. We took photos of it, hoping to catch Fireplace Dave! We made up plans at sleepovers about how to prove he was real!

And, even though we never proved it, right now (in the living room) it's hard not to think about almost-a-year ago, and the fluorescent lights buzzing, buzzing, buzzing.

The difference, this time, is that Shoelace isn't here.

Shoelace isn't here, and the moonglow-lanterns buzz and buzz and buzz.

CHAPTER 30

I pull my phone from my pyjama pocket. Shoelace still hasn't messaged back yet.

'Shoelace,' I hiss, because I want her more badly than in my whole entire life. I want to hear her voice. I want to feel her hand in mine. Plus it'd be really nice if Mum called back, too.

RoaryCat and Ben finally reach the end of the corridor, and it's like it comes from nowhere. The two of them enter a HUUUGE square-shaped hall taken up by another deep, deep swimming pool – one that's at least two, even three times the size as me and Shoelace's attempt in Mount Tuna Paste Mountain, and which makes even the biggest real-life pool feel like a piddly little puddle in comparison. The water is calm, and illuminated by the vast, lantern-littered ceiling.

I gasp at it. Gape at it.

How long would it take a player in Voxminer to build all of this?!

The tiles on the walls and ceiling are pale blue – yet the path that circles the entire span of the gargantuan swimming pool is tileless, and dark blue, and patterned with pictures of stars and fish and bubbles. It looks exactly like the carpet in my real-life bedroom.

I tremble and try very utterly hard not to look at the weird blue carpet that looks so much like the one in my room. But that leaves me gazing at the walls, and I don't like looking at them either, because the walls of that enormous space alternate between dark, shadowy exits and wide, tall windows. Through the windows, I spy that murky purple-brown glow you only see on cloudy city nights.

My breath catches and my heart catches and my literal soul catches.

I make RoaryCat and Ben sneak around the carpeted path to the nearest window. It's hard to make anything out through the sparkle-glass: some dark splodges that might be the backs of houses . . . some almost-black patches that might or might not be a jumble of lanes and gardens . . .

I clutch the GG5 controller so tightly that my fingers hurt.

'Shoelace,' I whisper – because what would Shoelace do?

But I already know because she'd have done it by now. She would've headed down one of the dozens of pitch-black exits that line the walls of the giant hall. The exits are square-shaped. Even though they don't have teeth or anything, they make me think of swallowing mouths.

Which swallowing exit do I go down?

'The one that's closest, silly,' I imagine Shoelace saying. 'If it's closest, that means it's the best!'

But I'm not Shoelace, and I'm not going to rush through the nearest exit just because it's there.

Ben sits neatly on the carpet. His ears droop. He curls his snowy tails round his icy body, and I want to stroke him through the screen.

'Ben,' I whisper. 'It's okay.'

Outside, the wind dies completely. The house falls so silent that all I hear is my own breath and heartbeat, and the lanterns on the TV with their never-ending buzz.

Is it too late to abandon Voxminer, rush upstairs and lock myself in my bedroom? Is it too late to leave the house entirely? Should I leave? Is it illegal for a not-quite-twelve-year-old to be out alone at night? Is that why Mum got so wound up about ground rule number eight??

In the end, even though I'm not Shoelace and I don't want to choose an exit at random, I don't know what else to do. I've got nooo idea if the exits all go to the same place or whether they just lead to a million dead ends, like a labyrinth.

More than that, I can feel something . . .

There's a tug, a tug on my heart, and I can't ignore it. It guides me to the shadowy exit closest, the one that Shoelace would probably take. And, even though it's just my imagination and doesn't make sense, the tug is the only thing that even resembles a clue about which exit to head down.

Ben whimpers on the dark blue carpet of the path around the swimming pool.

'Come on,' I say to him, softly. 'Let's go.'

Purple fear symbols flash over his head. He's not budging.

I huff. But then I think of something, and I've got no idea why I didn't think of it before.

'Fine,' I tell him. 'Fine! I'll get you some friends!'

Then I open up the Voxfriendopedia, and scroll through to find Ben some company.

Species	Squoo
Nickname (Optional)	Squishtastic
Biome	Reef
Level	52

Dazzles its enemies with its light-up tentacles. A swarm of squoos is called a squooshing, and a large enough squooshing can shine brighter than the twin moons.

Species	Smitten Bitten
Nickname (Optional)	Sir Augustus Horatio Palindrome
Biome	Candy fields
Level	29

Often mistaken for a clump of candyfloss, but don't be fooled: its liquorice claws aren't to be trifled with.

Species	Pantherlassa
Nickname (Optional)	Riley
Biome	Deep ocean
Level	61

A most ancient of Voxfriends, the oldest known pantherlassa

fossil is over 220 million years old! Uses its giant fangs to carve love poems on the seabed.

Species	Zoxen
Nickname (Optional)	SHOELACE LOOOOK I'M TYPING YOUR NAME
Biome	Night sky
Level	43

A rare Voxfriend that grazes off fresh moonlight on the peaks of midnight clouds. Its fearsome skeletal appearance belies its shy, thoughtful

personality.

Species	Illumamoth
Nickname (Optional)	mR SPARK SPARK
Biome	Pine forest
Level	59

According to tradition, those who see illumamoth shining among the trees on the eve of their birth will be blessed with a year and a day of good fortune.

MORE (Press D)

I can only have three Voxfriends out at once, except Ben's obviously not going anywhere, and Riley, my pantherlassa, is a must. That leaves only one other Voxfriend, and I can't decide between Squishtastic and mR SPARK SPARK. Both would be ultra extremely good at lighting the way through the dark. But though Squishtastic is a bazillion times better at swimming, mR SPARK SPARK has more powerful attacks.

In the end, it doesn't matter. Because, when I try selecting Riley, a message appears that I've never seen before. That I don't reckon anyone's ever seen before.

THIS VOXFRIEND IS AFRAID AND WILL NOT LEAVE THE INVENTORY

I try Squishtastic, but Squishtastic won't leave either, and neither will mR SPARK SPARK. Then I pick Voxfriends at random – my clock-o'-lantern, melody hare, magmazola.

It's the same message every time.

THIS VOXFRIEND IS AFRAID AND WILL NOT LEAVE THE INVENTORY

I take a deep breath, squeeze Jonesy, then imagine again that Shoelace is sitting right next to me, and that we're facing this together. I close the Voxfriendopedia.

'Sorry, Ben,' I whisper at the screen.

Ben whimpers again, but thank actual goodness that he

doesn't vanish and return to the Voxfriendopedia himself. He stands back up from where he's sitting and follows RoaryCat11 through the shadowy exit, away from the huge freakish hall with its giant swimming pool and weird carpeted path and all those windows filled with the purple-brown glow of a cloudy city night.

A short while into the darkness, we come across wet, dimly lit steps totally covered in grimy orange tiles. And the further down them RoaryCat and Ben head, the more the steps keep splitting, lightning-like, into even smaller, thinner, crampier, dingier, dirtier staircases—

stairs
that
twist
down
into
dark
stairs
twist
down
into
dark
stairs

twist

down **down**

into into

dark dark

stairs stairs stairs

twist twist twist

down **down** **down**

into into into

dark dark dark

stairs stairs stairs

twist twist twist

down **down** **down**

I find a web

of dark

grey

tunnels

that bend

and twist

and water

flows   flows

through   through

the tunnels   the tunnels

and   and

sometimes   sometimes

the tunnels   the tunnels
split   split   split
and then   and then   and then
sometimes   sometimes
the tunnels   the tunnels
join up once again
yet also
I've got
nooo idea
where
the tunnels
are leading me

then the tunnel I'm in widens and there's
a swimming pool and the pool's even bigger
than the one me and Shoelace made,
and from the green-blue water rise

columns columns columns

columns columns columns

columns columns columns

columns columns columns

columns columns columns

columns columns columns

they're like a half-sunken forest,
and even though this is a video game
I can pretty much smell the chlorine.
I basically taste it in my mouth.

Through wide sparkle-glass windows on the ceiling, I spy the murky purple-brown glow of a cloudy city night. And all round the walls of the green-blue swimming pool are dozens of little platforms that rise from the water. Each platform leads to a wooden door, and the doors lead to I don't know where. I don't know where.

So I do what Shoelace would: I pick a platform at random, then make RoaryCat and Ben swim right over to it. Then I make RoaryCat open the door there – it does so with a creak – and behind the door waits a black-tiled staircase, long and thin.

I bite a finger, then breathe out. I'm starting to hate swimming-pool tiles.

At the bottom of the narrow steps is another corridor, and the corridor is half flooded with strange black water. I can't see below the surface.

My fingers quiver on the GG5 controller because I recognise exactly where RoaryCat and Ben have found themselves.

It's a corridor from St Peter's.

It's the corridor where the Year Five and Year Six classrooms were.

CHAPTER 29

I think of me and Shoelace running away from Fireplace Dave, and my tummy squirms, and I want to curl up even tighter. I want to run from the house all the way to Shoelace's, or to Save Shoppers, and I don't even care that Mum would be properly mad with me.

Yet, in my bones, I know that whatever's happening has nothing to do with Fireplace Dave.

Fireplace Dave is a joke. A story you tell each other at school. Literally, his name is flipping Fireplace Dave.

And is it my imagination or does Ben look at me again – real-life me sitting frozen on the living-room carpet under the glow of the big light? He only does it for a second, then flicks his tails and turns back to RoaryCat. But, for that one split instant, I swear he was begging me to put down the GG5 controller and run from the living room.

However, I can't turn back. Not when I'm close.

What I'm close to, I don't know, but I can sense it, sense it in the electricity in my skin. Whatever is happening, the answer waits behind one of the classroom doors.

My fingers twitch.

'Don't do it,' I whisper to myself. 'Go upstairs. Wait for Mum.'

I'm powerless. I feel the tug, that strange little wisp of a tug, pull on my heart again. I tilt the joystick forward. RoaryCat wades through the flooded corridor.

'Lori!' I snap at myself. 'Turn back, Lori.'

But the tug gets stronger, and I wonder, suddenly, if maybe the feeling isn't what I assumed it was. I already knew it was strange, but I at least thought it was coming from me – from some deep-down-inside-me place I'd never known about until tonight.

What if it's not? What if the tug isn't coming from inside me? What if something in the game has hooked me like a fish on a line and is reeling me in?

The tug p u l l s ,

p u l l s ,

p u l l s . . .

A thrill of icy horror blasts through my body.

I wish Shoelace was here.

I wish she was here.

But she's not here, and I'm not as strong as her, and I can't resist the tug. All I can do is make RoaryCat and Ben pass by rows of plastic chairs, those ones with spindly metal legs that you only ever see in school. They're lined up neatly on both sides of the corridor, legs in the water and backs to the walls. All of them are empty. All of them watch RoaryCat as she wades on by.

The tug leads me to the door to my old Year Six classroom.

Not counting the buzzing moonglow-lanterns, it's quiet. A hear-your-own-heartbeat silence.

I clench my teeth.

Then I make RoaryCat open the door.

The place she and Ben enter, however, is not my old classroom.

My stomach twists as I try to make sense of it. The space is so utterly enormously titanically stupidly massive that Voxminer struggles to load it: an ocean of the same shallow water that floods the corridor, and the water's so smooth, calm and dark that it's like the biggest mirror in all entire existence. It reflects the black sky above completely perfectly, and the sky bursts with stars, and the stars are red as blood. Rising from the sea to the star-splattered sky are pale thin strands of what look like string, and the strands reach so high that I can't see where they come from. The dark sky just swallows them up.

The GG5 fan whirrs wildly.

It shouldn't. The Game Galaxy 5 is still unplugged. Yet the fan spins anyway as the console tries to load those tons of red stars and the black-mirror sea and the weird strands that reach up and up to the sky above – and I don't know what it is about them, but the strands make me shudder. They're spaced out far apart from each other, but there are LOADS of them.

I make RoaryCat investigate the nearest one. Up close, I see that it doesn't rise from the water after all, but rather, it dangles – dangles from the sky – and the end of it hangs a little bit over RoaryCat and Ben. It's actually kind of yellowish-looking. Almost like—

I gasp. I shudder.

It's the exact same colour as spiderwebs in Voxminer!

I look up at the other strands, and at the black sky and the bazillion red stars. But I don't spot any spiders, so instead I make RoaryCat stare straight ahead and try my best to ignore the strands.

'Keep going,' I mutter to myself. 'Keep going. Keep going. Keep going.'

The water comes up to RoaryCat's knees, and almost to the snowy fur of Ben's sparkling white underbelly.

Everything's so open. There's nowhere to hide.

It makes me feel exposed.

Makes me feel watched.

'Mum,' I whisper. I do it without thinking. 'Shoelace . . .'

The GG5 fan stops spinning. I don't even breathe. And the buzzing from the school corridor fades as RoaryCat and Ben head further and further into the lonesome, silent sea.

Then, way away in the darkness ahead, I spot something. Two somethings. Two little dots of shocking blue.

I flinch. Before I can even think the words Shade Girl, though, the pair of possibly-maybe-eyes vanishes, and I don't even know if I saw them at all, or dreamed them up because of how tense I am, how jump-and-shriek-ready I am.

'It was nothing,' I mutter. If I say it out loud, maybe I can make myself believe it. 'It was nothing. Nothing.'

That's all the time I get to worry about it, though, since there are things up ahead, lots of things – much closer than the gleaming-possibly-eyes, yet so shadowy, so dark against the black water and black, black sky, that it's no surprise I didn't spot them until now.

Whatever the things are, they don't move; they don't make any sound either. I move RoaryCat as close as I dare to them, and discover that, even though I didn't spot them until now, they're giant – taller than both Ben and RoaryCat. They stick out from the water, tons of them, HUNDREDS of them. They're clustered together as far as Voxminer can load them. They're round and smooth, almost like—

Eggs.

Dread coils round my ribs; the whispered words of my bedroom door suddenly pierce through my head. 'See how deep the egg nest goes,' the doorway said . . .

I gasp.

'Oh my goodness.'

I think of me and Shoelace building the Royal Egg House at the end of summer, then searching all over Kittentopia for nests of Voxfriend eggs.

'Let's look for a desert biome,' I remember Shoelace saying one time. 'Maybe we'll find some cactus-kitten eggs to bring back. That would be the COOLEST!' (Never mind that we didn't have any of the right tools or Voxfriends to survive in the desert. But we did it anyway, and RoaryCat11 almost got killed by a giant cactus-kitten mother.)

The eggs in the water aren't like any of the ones in the Royal Egg House – not just because they're huge and dark and patternless, but also their shells glisten wetly in the freakish red starlight. I've never seen eggs like them in my life.

A thought slams into me like a tidal wave.

I've made a mistake.

I could have turned back. I SHOULD have turned back. I should have done what Shoelace would have and battled the tug harder, that feeling of being drawn in like a fish on a line, and then I should've rushed upstairs and locked myself in my room with the lights on. Because, in my suddenly-cold-bloodstream, I am one billion per cent sure that obeying the tug was the absolute worst thing on earth I could ever in a million years have done tonight.

I feel my heart beat. Take the biggest breath of my utter life.

'Okay,' I whisper. 'Okay, okay, okay. Go. Go.'

I abandon Voxminer, jump to my feet, turn my back to the TV and face the living-room door instead, ready to fight the tug and make a run for it—

A noise cuts through the gargantuan hush.

It's small. It comes from behind, from the TV.

In the silence, it feels loud as

thunder.

Crack.

CHAPTER 28

I freeze, still clutching the GG5 controller. I don't look back. I absolutely do not look back at the TV screen, but keep my eyes firmly on the living-room door.

'Just go, Lori,' I tell myself. I speak so quietly that all I'm really doing is moving my lips up and down. 'To your room. Don't look at Voxminer.'

Crack.

But I have to look.

Crack.

Because I know what that sound is.

Crack. Crack.

Something is hatching.

I'm terrified to see what it is, yet somehow not knowing feels even worse. The tug tells me to look, look, look.

My heart beats, beats, beats.

Crack. Crack. Crack.

I feel Jonesy's softness against my chest, from where the little plush lion still pokes from the collar of my pyjama top. I imagine

Shoelace squeezing my hand superly tight.

Then I turn and face the TV again.

The massive eggs twitch on the screen. Jagged lines race across their shells like cracks in glass, and Ben half growls, half whines by RoaryCat's side. He's back in his attack position, ears flattened in terror. The black water turns to ice round his paws.

Voxfriends are NOT supposed to act like that. They are NOT meant to make you feel like they're actually-for-real terrified!

Yet I'm done pretending Ben is an ordinary Voxfriend.

I don't know how it happened, or when, or why. But, for some reason that makes no sense and which I don't understand at all, Ben is alive. He's alive, and he's watching out for me and trying to keep me safe.

'Oh my goodness,' I whisper to him. 'Ben. Get out of there.'

The eggs wriggle. Wriggling, writhing eggs as far as I can see.

I bite my lower lip because what do I do? Hide in my room until Mum gets back? But I can't shake the horrible knife of a feeling that, no matter where I am in the house, I'm not safe. That whatever is haunting me is waaay more dangerous than just a ghost in Voxminer.

Ben whimpers again.

The great ferocious blizzuar is watching out for me. Who's watching out for him?

'Ben,' I breathe. 'Move.'

What would Shoelace do?

She'd grab my shoulders, of course. She'd shake me and yell, 'Roars! Save him!'

crack crack crack

I hop up and down on my ruined blanket fort. Ben is alive, but the trouble is he's still a Voxfriend in a video game, which means he can't move by himself. All he can do is follow RoaryCat around, or I can return him to the Voxfriendopedia. Either way, he can't escape the endless black sea unless I make RoaryCat herself run from the eggs.

crack crack

crack

crack

Ben HOWLS.

Above me, in the living room, the light flickers again. Then it goes out completely, and the room is plunged into darkness.

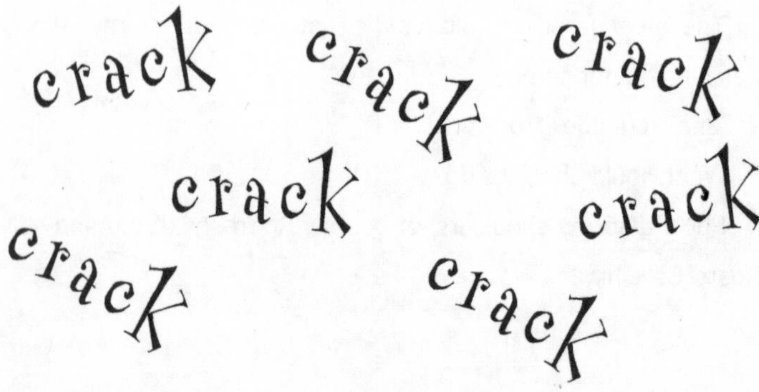

A surge of energy EXPLODES through me, and I've got nooo idea if it's fear or bravery or something else. Whatever the feeling is, it's cold, like I've been chucked outside in just my pyjamas. I'm suddenly more alert than any girl's ever been in all entire history.

And the tug on my heart is severed – that feeling that urged me deeper and deeper into the maze of swimming pools.

I FEEL the tug being severed, like whatever had its hooks in me has finally been torn loose! But even though I'm free to run, free to rush from the living room, I feel throw-uppy in my mouth.

I can't leave Ben. I can't leave him in that awful, horrible place.

With a groan, I make RoaryCat race back through the water, back towards the school corridor. The doorway stands in the black-mirror ocean, like a portal to safety. Yet the door isn't alone any more. Somehow, even though I'm completely certain that there weren't any there before, I spy at least a hundred new eggs in the space between RoaryCat and the lonely doorway, as though they spawned from nowhere when I wasn't looking.

Ben flicks his twin tails and follows RoaryCat – just as things emerge from the eggs.

I scream. Countless arms erupt from the shells, arms made from shadow and slime. They're peppered with teeny-tiny little stars, no bigger than pinpricks, and the pinprick stars are blinding.

The joystick digs into my thumb.

'Run!' I growl at RoaryCat, even though she's already going as fast as I can make her.

Then the eggs fall apart, and out of them flop children: children in dripping-wet rags, and all of them have that weird starry skin. If I could smell them through the screen, I bet they'd smell 100 per cent rancid.

I gag.

And, even with Voxminer's cartoon graphics, I know that the children are all girls, every last single utter one of them. I recognise as well that they're not just wearing any old rags, but that the rags used to be bright blue Voxminer pyjamas.

I know all this because, if you ignore their slimy, starry-night skin, all the children look like me.

Me! Lori! With my freckly face and long brown hair that reaches past my shoulders!

The newly hatched Loris stumble through the water. They're not as fast as Ben and RoaryCat, but there are a gazillion million of them, so they don't have to be fast. They just have to get in Ben and RoaryCat's way.

Hairs rise on my arms and legs.

The swarms of Loris surround Ben and RoaryCat and reach out with slime-dripping fingers—

'FASTER!' I screech.

Then, thank God, Ben and RoaryCat hurtle through the door that leads from the black-mirror ocean to the upstairs classroom corridor, and I make RoaryCat slam it behind them. Then I guide the two of them back to the mighty green-blue swimming pool with the dozens of columns in it—

Down the web of dark grey tunnels—

Up the twisting, grimy orange steps—

To the huge hall with the huge, huge swimming pool, where the ceiling shines with moonglow-lanterns and the walls are lined with windows and exits. And though I want to make RoaryCat carry on, back down the endless corridor to Mount Tuna Paste Mountain, there's no time. No time. It would take too long.

Because something is watching me. And I don't mean they're watching RoaryCat11, but me in the living room, in the gloom under the blown-out light.

I've got no idea what it is, but I can FEEL it watching.

I drop the GG5 controller on the carpet. 'Sorry,' I whisper to Ben. 'I think you'll be safe now, though.' My voice cracks. 'I hope so. Oh God. I don't know. I don't know what to do. Ben. What do I do?!'

Ben nods at me from the screen. It's like he's saying, Oh my complete and utter goodness, you've done more than enough for me. Run upstairs already!

Shakily, I return his nod, and, stopping only to yank Jonesy out from my collar and clutch him to my chest, I turn from the TV and don't look back. I open the living-room door. Hurl myself into the downstairs hallway.

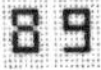

I.

Do.

Not.

Look.

Back.

Artwork to come

Where your name
gives me strength

CHAPTER 27

Thank goodness, thank total absolute goodness, it's only the living room where the light went out. I thunder upstairs and scream all the way since I can feel I'm being chased by something. Something dark. Something downright evil.

At the top of the stairs, I THROW myself into my bedroom, then spin round, ready to face whatever's after me.

Yet there's nothing there.

Nothing.

At.

All.

I shudder and back up against the wall, eyes locked on the empty staircase through the open door of my bedroom. Nothing was hunting me. It was in my head. All in my head. Me and Jonesy are completely alone.

But, though it turns out I wasn't really being chased, the being-watched feeling grows stronger every single second. And, despite what my eyes are telling me, I know the actual real truth. I know it in my bones.

We're not alone.

Whatever is watching me, it's invisible. Though I can't see it, I can SENSE it.

The air is boiling as August and stuffy as heck. Sweat trickles down my face, almost into my eyes. I'm scared to move.

But I've got to. I can't stay here with my back against the wall all night.

I gulp and turn to my bed–

My heart freezes all over again.

'Oh,' I whisper. 'Right . . .'

The duvet isn't there and neither are the sheets and pillows. They're in a heap in the living room, littered with Detective Mermaid comics and my drawing pad and my favourite Shimmer Squad book, all of them soaked in half a glass of spilled milk.

I dig my nails into my skin, then wipe my brow. Hot or not, stuffy or not, I need a duvet. The thought of curling up on an empty mattress, even one with the Sea Gang on it, makes me want to cry.

Through the doorframe, my gaze falls on Mum's bedroom down the landing. Her door is still open from earlier, plus her light is on, too . . .

I bite my lip. Squeeze Jonesy again.

I can do it.

I can run to Mum's room, slam the door and hide there until she gets back! My alarm clock says it's past ten already, which leaves less than an hour and a half until half past eleven – less than an hour and a half until she's home. It sounds like forever, but really that's just four-and-a-bit episodes of Monster Kitten Fighting Force.

It's doable, but only in the safety nest of Mum's bedroom.

My legs go tense.

'After three,' I whisper. 'Three . . . two . . . o-one . . .'

I run, I gallop, I HURTLE down the landing and comet into Mum's room! Then I SLAM the door behind me and twist the key in the lock and collapse against the door and cuddle Jonesy as hard as lionly possible. Behind me, through the door, I still sense the being-watched feeling. But I finally let myself smile, because even though I'm ultra-aware that I'm now right over the living room, somehow, in the warmth of Mum's bedroom, the being-watched feeling suddenly isn't even half as strong as it was just seconds ago.

Mum's wallpaper is yellow. Her queen-sized bed is covered in a flowery yellow duvet. Mum doesn't have posters, not like in my room, but she's got pictures of us in wooden frames in neat little rows on the walls. There are boxes and folders for boring old bank stuff, all arranged by year, month, week, day and – I swear – even by hour, minute and second. Mum. Is. Organised. She's even more organised than a pickpidge, aka a Voxfriend that looks like a pigeon and is the tidiest, neatest Voxfriend in the world.

The room smells of Mum. A fussy smell. A safe smell. It's a laundry scent, since she always has at least two clean uniforms for work.

The curtains are open, and orange streetlamps shine through the windows, and I can see out on to the street. It's empty. There's no one around, and I can't even see any lights on. But, like Jonesy and the weight of my phone in my pocket, the sight makes me calmer. It reminds me that, even though it feels like my house is the only single one in all existence, in reality, because we live on a terraced street, I'm just metres away from dozens of neighbours.

It's an odd thought but comforting. Because though I hardly even know them, and the very idea makes my tummy wriggle-squirm, as a final break-the-glass-in-case-of-emergency option, my neighbours are there for me.

My smile widens. I open the curtains more and stare and stare at the empty street.

There's one thing, though, that I don't like about Mum's room, and it's the weird little wardrobe room squished into the corner.

I glower at it. I've NEVER liked it: a strange sliver of a room behind a white wooden door, and with absolutely negative zero point whatsoever, since it's way too narrow to do anything useful with. Mum can barely even keep boxes in there – when she stacks up too many, the ones near the back become super hard to reach. It's not even good for hide-and-seek because it's too good! The one time I did use it as a hiding spot, Shoelace didn't find me for aaages, so long that it stopped being fun and started being boring instead. Then this great massive spider came out of nowhere and crawled right up the side of my leg, and it was like it was saying, 'HI, LORI! I'M HERE TO MAKE THINGS EXCITING AGAIN!!'

I grimace at the memory, brush at my leg, then pile boxes and folders against the wardrobe door. At first, I keep everything in order so that Mum won't lose her filing system. But then I think of big dirty spiders creeping about in the dark and start shoving boxes totally at random until half the door is covered and the wardrobe is as good as locked.

Finally, with the big light still on, me and Jonesy dive under Mum's duvet so that not even our heads poke out.

I curl on my side and smile again.

I'm safe.

Not 100 per cent safe-safe, but safe enough that, if I keep still and quiet until Mum gets back, I can cope.

Silence falls over the bed like an extra blanket.

There's one more thing I need to do.

I slip out my phone from my pyjama pocket; under the duvet, the screen is half blinding. But I squint my eyes, search for Mum in my contacts, then try her again.

Her phone goes straight to the answer-machine lady.

'I'm sorry, but the person you have called is not available. Please leave a message after the tone.'

I try again.

'I'm sorry, but the person you have called is not available.'

One more time.

'I'm sorry, but the person you have called is not available.'

I try Shoelace.

'I'm sorry, but Crazy Charlie Ruler of Penguins is not available.'

I try Dad.

'I'm sorry, but the person you have called is not available.'

I try Granddad, then Aunt Mae and my cousin Gregg and my other cousin Angus. For some reason, Beatrice-from-school is still in my contacts, even though we haven't spoken since Year Five – but I try her, too, just in case. I even call a weird number that rang me the other day, but which Mum reckons was a scam.

No matter who I call, and even though my phone insists I've got reception, I get the same response every single time.

'I'm sorry, but the person you have called is not available.
Please leave a message after the tone.'

CHAPTER 26

I leave voicemails for everyone, yet get a sinking feeling that no one's getting them. All I know for sure is I've got 25 per cent battery left, plus there's over an hour until Mum gets back.

At least I'm safe. I am safe. I am safe under Mum's duvet.

I hug Jonesy and check to see if Shoelace has replied to any of my messages. She hasn't even seen them, though, so I send her one more, just in case. A short one. A really short one.

I'm scared
Please call

I send the same to Mum, then stare at the message she left a few hours ago, reading the same little bit of it over and over.

Love you everything. Should still
be back at half eleven ⊠ xxxx

God, I wish she really was watching me through the phone camera right now.

I swallow. I don't know this feeling, this feeling in my stomach. It's like love, except I'm queasy; like fear, except there's hope. It's like being awake past midnight, too scared to fall asleep, yet being too old, now, to go and sleep with Mum. Except that, if only I hang on long enough, Mum will come to me instead.

A light flicks on in my head.

The Voxminer forums.

Could I post online about all this? Could I ask someone to call Mum for me, then get her to come home early? Would that be crazy?

The instant I visit the forums, though, I can tell something's off. They don't load properly. They only half load. I see pictures, but no comments, no usernames, no writing at all.

Frustration wriggles in my belly. My phone is as slow as a slumberjaw, the sleepiest Voxfriend in Voxminer. Even on normal nights, I always expect stuff like this to happen.

It's never this slow, though, my mind hisses at me.

(I scowl. I wish my mind would just shut up sometimes.)

The battery's at 22 per cent. I think about putting the phone on sleep, but hesitate, then turn the screen brightness down and keep on browsing.

I can't call anyone. Shoelace isn't seeing my messages. I can't write to anyone on the Voxminer forums.

But perhaps I can still find answers. Has anyone else ever seen the black-mirror sea with the eggs in it? Does the sea have something to do with Shade Girl?

Almost at once, I crash into another problem: just like the forums, I can't find a search engine that'll load. Hookline. Ask Poodle.

Breadcrumb. None of them work.

My stomach knots. So I start trawling through Voxminer fansites instead, hunting for anything that might help, anything at all. Thankfully, oh thank actual goodness, this time, the sites load just fine.

(On a whim, I open another tab and shoot back to the Voxminer forums. But they're still broken, the one site I super ultra-need.)

After a while, I find an article on vmfacts.com that tells me everything I could ever learn about Shade Girl, where she came from and how she got popular. It even shows part of the weird old comic everyone knows about, that has a picture of her blank face and bright blue eyes staring, staring.

Shade Girl

Comments: 993

She Watches redirects here

Tagged in community history and 6 other categories

Last edited 4 weeks ago by LuckyDreams2012

<insert shade girl illustration>

This page describes a fan-made creation. Shade Girl has never appeared in any official version of Voxminer. Hence none of the details on this page should be considered canon.

UPDATE: Comments on this page have been temporarily locked. For more information, see community guidelines.

Shade Girl is a paranormal entity created by Illumamoth-shining-bright on 15 February 2012, on the now defunct voxleaf.net. Since her inception, Shade Girl has gained significant fame both within and outside the fandom, and is considered Voxminer's unofficial mascot. She has frequently been acknowledged by Wolf and Tiger Studios.[1] She was also the subject of an international incident involving the Chancellor of the United Kingdom.[2]

<D>Table of voxtents

History

Please note that, although the following represents a best attempt to piece together a timeline, omissions are not only possible but probable. In particular, numerous community-led efforts to track down and interview Illumamoth-shining-bright have resulted in failure, meaning that the true motivation behind their creation might never be uncovered.

<C>Original voxleaf.net post

On 13 February 2012, in response to the recent release of Voxminer Version 1.1, Voxleaf user Gotz2GoDeeper posted a thread detailing why they considered the newly introduced blizzuar to be a superior Voxfriend to community favourite power fox.[3] This caused a heated discussion, with many Voxleaf users weighing in to voice their opinion.

On 15 February 2012, presumably taking advantage of the unusual amount of attention the thread was receiving, user Illumamoth-shining-bright posted a comment derailing the original premise of the discussion.

They wrote of playing Voxminer on their Game Galaxy 3 while home alone. They had been creating a shopping mall when they chanced upon a mysterious door that they had no memory of building. Through the door was a lengthy hallway leading to a second shopping mall that, again, they insisted they had never seen. In the second mall was a being named Shade Girl. The being was 'made from shadow', had bright blue eyes, and subsequently vanished into thin air before Illumamoth-shining-bright could take a closer look.[4]

<C>**BigFunPunPossum stream**

Amused by the novelty of the post, many users abandoned the blizzuar/power fox debate and began discussing Shade Girl instead. The tale seemed to especially resonate with a particular handful of users, who vehemently insisted that they themselves had had similar experiences, and had encountered the same entity described by Illumamoth-shining-bright.[5] Three such users – 4evaInMyKnee, dirttrackSam and BigFunPunPossum—

I stop reading. It's partly because most of this isn't useful, but mostly because the details that do hit home hit a little too hard: a mysterious door; a basically endless hallway; others insisting they'd experienced the exact same thing. Plus learning about how Illumamoth-shining-bright made just one single post about Shade Girl on a now-dead website, then was never heard from again makes my skin prickle. It makes my whole entire soul prickle.

Somehow, one thing I've never seen before is the actual post they wrote. I mean, it's famous, but I've never actually read it or anything.

Luckily, it was screenshotted before voxleaf.net went down.

I find it in the vmfacts gallery. I stare at the date on it: 15 February 2012.

There's something different about reading the date in an article versus seeing it in the actual real-life post itself. The post is old. As in from before I was born old. It's easy to forget Voxminer has been around for even longer than me and Shoelace.

A frown creeps over my face as I read on. I don't fully understand it. I don't get why Illumamoth-shining-bright wrote so . . . oddly.

Yet, thanks to the article, I understand enough for shivers to squiggle through my skin.

[-] ⊠ !!Illumamoth-shining-bright 15/02/12 (Wed) 21:17:41 No. 1647947

File: jellyspoonface.jpg (48 KB, 387x335)

<insert Shade Girl artwork>

artwork to come

>be me, 16

>am alone in house, turn on GG3 start Voxminer

>be building a shopping mall

>lol wut who put this random door here? not me

>open door

>find hallway. Goes on forever, srs who made this?

>creepedout.jpg

>go down hallway, find second mall I didn't build

>mall is HUGE

>louds of colums. Is like maze

>WHO BUILD THIS I DID NOT BUILD THIS?!?!

>feel am being watched

>spot figure by colums

>girl.jpg?

>girl be made from shadow

>girl be watching me.. Watches me through the screen

>I FEEL her watching. Her eyes glow blue

>I watch her back then she vanish into nothing. she gone

>nope nope nope nope

>my best voxfriend illumamoth appear frm nowhere. looks at me through scren

>illumamoth (thir name be Petrie) whispers "u in danger, shade girl comes

>doorbell rings, I jumping

>run downstairs. Older brother home frm work

>"bro Shade girl is after me"

>drag bro to tv

>wierd mall gone in Voxminer tho. Am back in overworld. Is sunny

>search everywher for mall, where it go???/

>bro laughs punchs my sholder. he say "love ya tons but u so weird lololol"

That's how I know Voxminer be haunted by Shade gril

this happen any1else??

I actually recognise a few of these phrases – 'WHO BUILD THIS', 'girl.jpg?' and 'this happen any1else??'. People use them in the Voxminer forums. They're jokes. Ooolllddd jokes. I never knew they all came from the exact same post.

The vmfacts gallery shows more ancient screenshots of people building on Illumamoth-shining-bright's original post. In one response, someone called historical_giant_crab decides that Shade Girl only comes out at night, and only when you're alone. In another, a user named beyondmice&evil swears up and down that, actually, they've seen Shade Girl, too, and that Shade Girl turned their inventory into swamp gunk, and look! Look! Check out this superly blurry photo that honest-to-God proves it!

I go back to the article. It explains how, like a game of whispers over ten years long and between who even knows how many Voxminer fans, Shade Girl as everyone knows her is born. The article links to comics! Fanfics! Livestreams where players faked seeing her! And, naturally, 'Shade Girl Throws Shade' and 'My Dinner With Shade Girl', two of the absolute most famous videos in the whole entire fandom. The moment Shade Girl went from being a small little in-joke in Voxminer to being known by everyone, ever.

Again, I don't care about any of that stuff. I only care about what Illumamoth-shining-bright wrote. If I'd seen their post earlier today, I would've laughed at it and messaged it to Shoelace.

Now, reading it makes gooseflesh bubble over my body.

It's the details.

Not just the door and the hallway, but the things the vmfacts.com article doesn't mention. The columns! How the second shopping mall felt like wandering through a maze! The fact that one of their Voxfriends warned them to turn back! And, sure, they didn't mention any swimming pools. But maybe Shade Girl looks at whatever you happen to be building at the time, then makes a nightmare version of it? Something like that?

The post looks like a joke. Everyone else thinks it's a joke. Yet the more times I read it, the more certain I am that Illumamoth-shining-bright was telling the truth. That maybe the real reason they posted somewhere popular was for the same reason I want to post on the Voxminer forums: that they were scared.

My hands tremble. I need to know more. I've got to know more. But, like the article says, Illumamoth-shining-bright never wrote anything else ever again.

I curl up tighter under Mum's duvet.

Then my phone beeps, and I jerk upright. My excitement dies again at once, though, because it's not Mum or Shoelace. No, it's a message saying the battery's at 5 per cent, and that the phone will go to sleep soon.

Great. Terrific. Just what I need.

I whisper a word that would get me into sooo much trouble if Mum heard me say it. Yet if I can't say it now, then when?

My charger's in my room, in the plug socket by my bed.

It might as well be at Shoelace's. Or on Mars. Or in Kittentopia itself.

I am NOT going back to my room. I'm not even going to look for a charger in Mum's room. Until she's back from work, no force on Planet Earth can make me slip out from under the duvet.

I hold Jonesy and stare at the battery symbol in the corner of the phone screen. The symbol is red. Next to it, it says 5 per cent.

4 per cent.

A tingle shoots through my skin.

Mum, please. Please come home. Oh God. Please.

3 per cent.

I draw in a deep breath. Then I brace myself, and switch off the phone to save the battery.

The screen goes black.

'Mum,' I whisper again. 'Come home early. Please.'

CHAPTER 25

Twenty to eleven isn't the latest I've ever been up, but it's almost the latest. As late as it can get before I start feeling properly naughty for not going to bed.

My eyes burn. My arms are heavy and so are my legs. But even in the bubble of safety of Mum's bedroom, I don't dare fall asleep, don't dare give in to tiredness.

. . . Maybe I shouldn't have hidden under the duvet . . .

With the heating up, it's a nest of warmth. It's too soft. Too comfy. Plus the bed smells like Mum, and I can pretty much pretend she's here right now, cuddling me.

I twitch.

Shoelace should be here, too. I wish me and Shoelace could be littler again and playing pretending games, drawing on Mum's tablet and watching funny videos online.

From nowhere, I remember when Shoelace first slept over after school. We turned my bed into a tent, then dared each other to stay in it for the whole entire evening. We were going to break The Record for how long two girls could stay in a really tiny space together. We even kept a minute-to-minute diary!

Mum brought us dinner in the tent, and we only gave up on The Record when, three hours and fifty-seven minutes in, Shoelace spilled mashed potato on the sheets. We laughed about it for ages.

It was so warm in that tent with Shoelace . . .

It's warm under Mum's duvet.

My eyes burn.

I want Shoelace. I miss Mum and Shoelace.

It's so warm.

I hug Jonesy.

I miss Mum.

It's warm under the duvet, and the duvet smells like Mum.

The bell rings for school.

I miss Shoelace.

Everyone gets into their seats.

The duvet smells like Mum.

I miss Shoelace.

Everyone has their exercise books. It's warm under the duvet, and the duvet smells like Mum. I smell paper, pencil shavings and a freshly mopped floor. It's the smell of Year Six.

It's warm under the duvet.

I miss Mum.

I miss Shoelace.

Shoelace is sitting next to me. She's in her uniform, in her school chair in Mum's bedroom.

Ms Newt tells everyone to settle down, then says, 'If you turn your swimming books to page twelve, you'll see that the water keeps rising. Keeps rising. It keeps on rising.'

I sit up in bed and turn my swimming book to page twelve. There's a graph with a scarlet line that goes up and up. Everything under the line is shaded blue.

My breath shakes.

Something is wrong.

I miss Shoelace.

I glance at Shoelace on my right. Her eyes are fixed on Ms Newt, and Ms Newt is using the interactive whiteboard on Mum's wall. It's warm under the duvet, and the duvets smells like Mum. The board shows a picture of my street. The street is flooded. The flood reaches to the first-floor windows.

I gulp and clutch at Mum's duvet.

I'm in my pyjamas. I'm in my bright blue Voxminer pyjamas at school.

Panic flares through me. Oh God, why am I in my pyjamas at school?! I hope Ms Newt doesn't notice I'm in my pyjamas under a warm duvet in bed. She'll tell Mum. Mum will be mad at me.

Slowly, so that Ms Newt doesn't notice, I wrap Mum's duvet round myself to hide my pyjamas.

The air is hot but my stomach is ice. The duvet is warm. It's warm under the duvet, and the duvet smells like Mum.

Shoelace puts her hand up.

Ms Newt points at her. 'Shoelace?' she says.

'Ms, if the water keeps rising, keeps rising, does that mean we're not going to the swimming pool later?'

Ms Newt chuckles. 'Gracious, but of course we are! I trust you all remembered your swimming costumes?'

'Yes, Ms Newt!' the class choruses.

I glance around and everyone is dressed for the pool, and so is Shoelace. Everyone is at their desks in trunks and swimsuits, and water laps at their feet, but no one notices. No one seems bothered by how boiling it is. No one winces at the stench of chlorine.

I need to leave. I need to go to my room and change into my swimming costume. But I can't risk Ms Newt spotting me in my pyjamas.

I'm sweating.

Something is wrong. The bed is scratchy. The water is up to everyone's knees.

Ms Newt claps her hands. 'Now, I trust you remember Illumamoth-shining-bright?' she says. She taps the whiteboard. A picture of a massive shopping centre in Voxminer appears, and the shopping centre is totally flooded. 'She was twelve, for the record, not sixteen as she claimed – my Hazel, dear Hazel. As it happens, she did find my door again, though only after her brother left her alone once more. Hazel didn't know it, but her brother's love was a shield. I could never stand love. I could never stand its light. But, with her older brother gone, Hazel was mine for the taking.

'You thoroughly proved yourself tonight, Lori,' Ms Newt continues. 'Do you know how many children make it as far as you into the labyrinth? You are one in ten million! You possess all the qualities I most value for the brood! You have suitable flesh, a suitable mind, and your body will make for fine feeding indeed.'

She smiles at me and her smile is hungry.

'Strong Lori. I can't say how pleased I am that you've proved your worth for the brood.'

I'm heaving, heaving. I wish Ms Newt would stop smiling at me. What's she banging on about 'the brood' for? Isn't that something to do with eggs? Hatchlings? Spiderlings?

I hug Jonesy more. In my gut, I know that what Ms Newt is saying is very, very, VERY important. Yet, for the absolute life of me, I can't figure out why.

Shoelace turns in her chair and looks at me. Everyone looks at me in Mum's bed – and, God, they've spotted that I'm wearing pyjamas, and they can see me hugging Jonesy too.

Never mind what a brood is. When Ms Newt tells Mum about this, Mum. Is going. To freak.

But where can I hide Jonesy? Where can I shove my special little lion doll so no one will see him?

Desperate, I grab Mum's duvet to stuff Jonesy under it. Then I crease my brow, confused, since the duvet feels scratchier than ever, like how sugar-sand in Voxminer would feel if sugar-sand was real. Plus the mattress is scratchy too.

Something is wrong. Something is very incredibly wrong.

A split second before I see it, my eyes widen because somehow – I have nooo idea how – I know precisely what I am about to see. But, even knowing the horrible thing that I am about to encounter, I lift Mum's duvet all the way up and look.

Eyes stare back at me.

They're made from fabric, and tattered, and sewn directly into the underside of the duvet: they've appeared all over the mattress, too, dozens of them, and they GLARE at me. They seem almost human, except their irises are bright blue cotton and their pupils scraps of black velvet. They are all different sizes, some small and grouped together, while others are bigger than my palm. A handful are large enough that I could sit cross-legged on them.

They all blink at the same time – blink with white woollen eyelids.

They are hungry for me.

Terror DETONATES through my muscles and

I scream

scream

SCREAM.

I screech so loudly that my throat is shredded to rags! I hurl Jonesy from the bed, scramble to get away—

My legs tangle in Mum's duvet—

I trip—

Smack against the mattress—

The tattered eyes follow me–

'MUM, MUM, MUM!'

I untangle myself, shove the duvet away–

'MUM, HELP, HELP!'

The eyes want to hurt me, HURT me. I tumble from the bed–

THWUNK.

I crash face first on the floor, and my skull erupts with lightning. But I have to get away. I have, I have to get away right this instant, instant–

I hurl myself against Mum's wall–

Turn round. Glare at the bed–

The eyes have vanished.

I breathe so hard that it hurts. Ms Newt is gone, too, and so is Shoelace and the rest of Year Six, and the water sloshing over the floor has disappeared as well. The big light shines over Mum's normal, familiar bedroom.

I rub the aching lump that swells on my forehead.

**'SHOELACE! WHERE ARE YOU?
SHOELACE! *CHARLIE!*'**

She was here! She was here in her red two-piece, sitting in her school chair on Mum's carpet! I know she was here! I SAW her!

'SHOELACE!'

I feel my pulse in my fingers. I lean against the wall, wondering desperately where Shoelace is hiding.

Realisation trickles into my head.

It wasn't real. None of it was real. It was a dream, all of it.

Yet the dream felt as real as real life! I can still taste the chlorine. I have NEVER had such a vivid-feeling dream before.

Just to be certain, I inch towards the bed and give the mattress a careful prod, ready for the eyes to reappear and stare me down again with those ragged hideous pupils. But the mattress just lies there, all innocent. Mum's yellow duvet sprawls half on the bed, half on the floor, and Jonesy has ended up by the door to the landing.

I snatch him up. Squeeze him to my chest. 'Sorry I threw you,' I whisper to him.

Then I collapse against the wall and sob into his mane.

CHAPTER 24

I'm going to leave the house.

Sure, Mum's clock says it's ten past eleven, and even though it's not raining any more I bet it's totally freezing outside, cold enough that there are probably frazil bears from Voxminer scampering about on their icy little paws. Plus I'm still worried it's illegal for a not-even-twelve-year-old to be out alone at night.

But never mind all that, or that Mum will be back soon: I can't stay here even a second longer. It's break-the-glass-in-case-of-emergency time.

Quickly, I glance around, thinking that I should charge my phone for at least the teensiest bit possible while I get my stuff together. Yet I can't find Mum's charger anywhere, and anyway I'm distracted by her curtains.

They are shut.

My heart pounds. I don't remember shutting them. I don't open them, though, I don't even go near them, but I unlock Mum's door again and fling it wide, wide open, then race to my bedroom.

Ms Newt's words ring in my head.

'Your body will make for fine feeding indeed.'

What.

Does.

That.

MEAN?!

I reach my room, slam the door behind me, and the first thing I notice is that the curtains here, too, are shut.

Were they closed before?

My head's still sleep-fuzzy. I don't remember.

Either way, the queasiness in my stomach says to stay well-the-heck away from them. Instead, I toss Jonesy on my bed, grab my Detective Mermaid schoolbag from under my homework desk and empty it over the floor. Then I shove socks and knickers into it, along with T-shirts and joggers and my newish swimming costume. Enough clothes that I'll never need to come home ever again.

Then I actually think about never coming home, and my heart goes faster and my breath goes shallow, and I stuff in some Shimmer Squad books and a notepad and the Monster Kitten pencil case that has all my colouring pencils and scented gel-pens and my dolphin-themed safety scissors in it. Any random little object in reach. Anything to remind me of my room. Of home.

Then I stop and take a deep breath, and go to rip my phone charger from the wall – except it's not there. It's not in the extension under the desk either, or in the weird, awkward plug socket by my bedroom door.

Is it downstairs? Or maybe I did leave it at Shoelace's?

I don't think so, though. And suddenly it feels kind of weird that I couldn't find Mum's charger either. Shouldn't I have been able to find at least one of them?

'It's – it's just in the kitchen or something,' I say to myself. I keep my voice low. It feels risky to talk too loudly. 'You don't need it, Lori. You're not going to be outside for long.'

I swallow, then grab Jonesy and press his nose against mine. Then into the bag he goes, and I zip it up and strap it tight over my shoulders.

Really, I should change out of my pyjamas first – except I am absolutely NOT undressing in this house where I can feel something watching me every single utter second. I'll put some clothes on over my pyjamas once I'm outside. Or, better yet, I'll just change at Shoelace's. She should be back from her aunt's party by now. And if she's not I'll wait outside for however long it takes.

In my heart, I know I shouldn't go to Shoelace's. I should knock on one of my neighbours' doors, or try and catch Mum on her way back from work. But what if she walks a different way from usual and I miss her? What if she gets a taxi for once? Also, Shoelace's is closer than Save Shoppers, plus Shoelace has the added advantage of not being one of my neighbours who I don't know and who probably won't believe me.

Plus I really need to see Shoelace. As in really, really need to see her.

I need her. I need her with my literal heart and all my actual soul.

From nowhere, I remember sleeping round hers near the end of

June, on her birthday; it was when she was properly getting back into Voxminer, and she was trying to get me back into it, too. (I mean, we've ALWAYS been into it because EVERYONE'S into Voxminer – it's basically pretty much the law! But you go through phases of playing-it-a-bit versus playing-it-a-ton, and we were both tipping into another ton-playing phase.)

We were in her massive new house, we had our sleeping bags rolled out in one of the airy big rooms downstairs, and the only other things set up were a rug and the TV and a fancy sofa and a small sorry house plant stuffed in the corner. She had her Game Galaxy 4 out, we had sweets and cola and takeaway pizza, and she was trying to eat pizza and play Voxminer at the same exact time.

I giggled, and my giggle echoed in the huge enormous room.

'Why do you keep turning your pizza upside down?' I asked.

Shoelace grinned at me. I noticed tomato sauce was smeared on one of her cheeks.

'Have I taught you nothing?' she said. 'You can't eat pizza the normal way, Roars. That's illegal.'

'Why's it illegal?'

'Duh. Cos then you don't get all the flavour, of course!'

She took another slice of pizza – not from the takeaway box, but from a plastic toy Voxminer sword I'd bought her for her birthday. I'd tied rainbow-coloured shoelaces round the hilt. She loved it. And, when the pizza arrived, she'd started using the flat blade of the sword as a makeshift dish.

She took another bite, turning her pizza upside down and stuffing it in her mouth before any toppings could drop on the rug.

Curious, I grabbed another slice myself and followed her lead – and, I swear, Shoelace was right: she was completely, totally right about the flavour—

Something creaks on the landing.

I gasp and stare at my bedroom door, still shut. But then the house falls quiet again, and I think it must have been the pipes. Or the floorboards? Mum says that, in old houses like ours, the wood can sometimes make weird sounds. Something to do with moisture? Temperature? Something-something science-science?

I clutch my beating heart.

Mercifully, the house stays quiet. So I scribble a note to tape to the front door.

<insert mum letter>

Artwork to come

I use my most extrally special blue paper with the shiny blizzuars round the edges. There's no way Mum will miss it!

My arms tremble. My breath trembles, too. It's all well and good telling Mum to call me, but how am I going to explain things over the phone without sounding like I've totally gone and lost it? How am I meant to explain things to Shoelace's parents when I show up randomly on their doorstep in the middle of the night?

Will they believe me?

Will Shoelace believe me?

My heart thumps madly. Of course she'll believe me. She's – she's Shoelace.

I grip the door handle, take a deep breath, then – wishing I had something sharp and pokey, even just a plastic toy Voxminer sword – I leave my bedroom.

My stomach seizes up.

Something's off. Something has changed, but I don't know what.

It's only halfway down the stairs that I realise what's wrong.

'Oh God,' I whisper. My head shakes back and forth. 'No, no, no, no, no-no-no.'

I must be dreaming still – I must be, I MUST be – yet I feel in my gut that this isn't a dream. I grip the banister, and the banister is solid, and the air is stifling from the heating being on max all night. This is definitely one billion per cent not a dream.

The front door is gone.

Not just missing from its frame, but gone entirely, like there was never a door there at all.

Just a wall.

CHAPTER 23

There's nothing odd-looking about the wall-where-the-front-door-should-be. It's covered in tired old wallpaper, the same yellowish-cream as most of the rest of our house. Yet it's the absolute non-weirdness of it that makes me sweat all over.

That wall shouldn't be there at all.

'What is this?' I whisper.

But I shut my mouth since the being-watched feeling crushes the breath from my lungs. Part of me feels I should creep up to the wall-that-shouldn't-be-there and press my hands against it to see if it's as real as it looks. Yet every last entire single instinct in my whole body stands on end and screeches – God, screeches! – at me not to go anywhere even CLOSE to it.

I think of fishhooks. I think of spiderwebs waiting for insects to get stuck and tangled in them.

On the whole, I think my instincts are prooobably right about this one.

Gulping, I take the final step down the staircase. I do it slowly because it dawns on me that something else has changed as well.

The silence. The silence is different from before.

It's the light.

I swallow and peer at the light that dangles in the downstairs hallway, with its frilly yellow shade that's got little pink flowers on it. It looks exactly the same as always.

It does not, however, sound the same.

It buzzes like the fluorescent lights from primary school, a noise like angry wasps – one of those sounds you don't notice at first, but that, once you do, burrows into your ears, and you wonder how on total earth you ever missed it in the first place. It's so LOUD.

Sick in my belly, I look away from the light, away from the wall-that-shouldn't-be-there. My vision falls on the open door of the kitchen.

A thought glimmers in my mind.

The garden.

I can escape through the kitchen, out into the garden, then to the back lane and freedom! And, sure, the big gate to the back lane has long since rusted shut, so that miiight be a bit of a problem. But, if I try, I reckon I can just about manage to climb over it . . .

I hum the Monster Kitten Fighting Force theme for bravery, then stride into the kitchen. Yet my heart sinks into my absolute stomach when I discover it's not just the front door that's missing but the back door, too. In its place is a patch of the kitchen's yellow wallpaper, newer, brighter, more cheerful than the rest of the house. My light brown wellies with otters on them are shoved lazily against the muddy skirting board. There's a pinboard with letters from school on it, and the pinboard's got photos of me, Mum and Shoelace at the beach this past summer, posing, smiling, having fun.

I don't keep my wellies in the kitchen – I've never kept them in the kitchen – but next to the shoe rack by the front door. I haven't ever seen that pinboard before either.

(Quickly, I glace around for a phone charger. But no luck because of course no luck.)

The kitchen light buzzes, and the buzz is lower than the one in the school corridor. It stuffs me with utter dread.

I sneak up to the new wall, brush the wallpaper with my fingers, feel the tough plaster beneath. You'd swear the wall had been there forever. Yet even though the back door is gone, plus the kitchen windows, too, there's still a draught coming from somewhere, although not a normal one. Draughts are supposed to be cold. This draught, however, is warm: a warm, thin breeze blowing from who-even-knows-where?

The wasp-buzz squirms under my skin.

Very, very slowly, I turn on the spot.

Take every Voxfriend in existence! Take every new Shimmer Squad novel before they're even out yet! I'd give all of it up to be literally anywhere else than in my house. Because, in the kitchen corner, there's another door, old and brown and battered, and which I always try to ignore since it's one of those doors that's creepy even in the daytime. It screams, 'Look at me, look at me! I'm absolutely haunted!'

It's the door to the cupboard under the stairs.

It rattles.

Not very much, but I gasp and jump back: since when do warm

breezes blow from cupboards under the stairs?!

The door shakes harder.

Something's wrong. The wrongness is in my bones and bleeds into my stomach. It gets worse and worse the more I stare at the rattling door.

Yet the absolute wrongest thing of all is that something deep in my heart kind of wants to open that hideous door. Part of me coos at me to turn the handle, then hurry on through and see where it takes me.

Do it, Lori, says the deep-inside part of me. You're wasting time. Open the door before it's too late.

I swallow and fidget on the spot. Why part of me thinks opening the cupboard door is even remotely a Good Idea™, I've got no clue at all. But the urge is easy to ignore since all the rest of me would rather lick up the milk-and-cookie mush currently soaking into the living-room carpet. I'd rather lock myself in Mum's creepy wardrobe room and let huge exciting spiders crawl over my skin and have a disco party in my hair. Most of me would rather do ANYTHING then go anywhere even near the cupboard under the stairs.

So I ignore the deep-inside part of me and hurry to the dining room. The light there buzzes, too, and the window is gone. But in its place is a big framed photo of me, Mum and Dad at the park, in the green shade of one of the willow trees by the lake. Mum's hair is way shorter than it is today – it barely reaches past her shoulders, and it's darker, and almost kind of cool looking. She's beaming. Dad's squatting beside her with his old rucksack on, the one with the keychain of a lion attached to the zip, which I always used to try and play with whenever he put the rucksack down. Mum's holding up my head so that I'm facing the camera. I must be about two or something.

The wrongness twists in my guts.

Mum doesn't keep any photos of Dad any more, let alone put them in frames, let-alone-let-alone hang them on the wall. Plus we didn't even live here when I was little. So how can we be at a park I never set foot in until I was seven? How can this photo exist?!

I don't bother checking the living room, but tear back upstairs because I'm going to do what Mum always says to do in a fire: shove my mattress through my window, then jump down on it so that I don't break a leg. Yet, when I rip open my bedroom curtains, all I find is my navy wallpaper with patterns of dolphins and starfish and whales and narwhals.

'Oh, come on!' I hiss, then rush to the bathroom.

No windows. Just yellow-cream tiles.

I check Mum's room.

No. Windows.

I pause and breathe and think and think and think.

My neighbours. My neighbours who I don't know and have never spoken to. They're my last final hope in the actual world.

I pound at the wall above Mum's bed, the yellow wall that separates one house from another. 'HELP!' I scream, then pick up Mum's heaviest receipt folder and bash that against the wall, too. 'IT'S LORI NEXT DOOR! HELP ME!'

But after a minute, or perhaps ten minutes, or a million, it's totally obvious I'm wasting my time. Nobody answers my screams. No one rings the front doorbell to see if I'm OK.

(Wildly, I think how tonight would've gone if Jesse the babysitter had checked up on me – 'Around nine,' as Mum had asked him. Would I still be pounding on the wall right now? Would everything in Voxminer have gone back to normal, the way it did for Illumamoth-shining-bright when her brother got home from work? Would I be like BigFunPunPossum, insisting to strangers online that I saw Shade Girl, that I honestly saw her for literally real?)

In the sweaty air all around, I sense the being-watched feeling.

I throw up my hands.

'I DON'T KNOW WHAT YOU ARE,' I scream at whatever is watching me, **'BUT YOU CAN'T KEEP ME HERE! LET ME OUT!'**

I miss Mum

I miss Shoelace

I miss Shoelace

I miss Shoelace

the lights buzz buzz

the buzz is in my head

it burrows in my skin.

YOUR BODY WILL MAKE FOR FINE FEEDING INDEED.

Suddenly I'm so, so aware of my whole entire body, of every last part of myself, as I race from Mum's room and back across the scorching landing. I feel my heart in my ribs, and I feel my lungs swell, and my stomach churns and my fingers tingle. My bare feet sweat against the carpet. Chills run through my legs and dance over the smooth skin of my tummy, then up my back and round my belly button.

I love my body.

I've never thought about it before, not like this, but I love my body, I love the body I live in, I love being a girl. I want to cry. I'm always saying to Mum that I'm nearly twelve, and twelve is almost a teenager. Yet, in my heart of heart of hearts, I love how short I am. I love being a kid since being one means that, if I wanted to – if I reeeeally wanted to and ignored the voice in me that says I'm almost nearly an almost-a-teenager – I could still sneak into bed with Mum. I could still cuddle up with her after having a nightmare.

Dear actual God, I haven't done that in a million years. But I want to. I want to. My breath catches. I want it more badly than anything else in the universe. The only thing I want more is Shoelace with me.

Halfway down the stairs, I stop and peer at the wall where the front door should be. The frilly ceiling light buzzes its freakish buzz.

I glower at the empty downstairs hallway.

'I'm not scared of you,' I whisper at whatever is watching me. 'I'm not scared.'

I'm blatantly lying, of course. But I say it anyway because, right then, I decide I'm going to do whatever it takes to see Mum again. I'm going to see Shoelace again, and I'm going to hold her hand and never let go of her – artist, pizza genius, my best friend in the world.

I don't know how, but I am going to get OUT of here.

CHAPTER 22

Mum's clock says half eleven: time for her to get back and discover the front door is missing.

I have to get hold of her. I need to let her know I'm trapped inside with no way out.

I reach for the phone in my pocket. Steady my hands. Switch it on.

The screen loads up. Instantly, the battery goes from 3 per cent to 2 per cent, and my stomach lurches. But I pull up my contacts and call her.

Her phone doesn't ring. It doesn't even go to the answer-machine lady. It does nothing whatsoever.

I'm about to hang up and dial 999, aka the one number I didn't try earlier. Yet, at the last split millisecond, finally, FINALLY, I hear something through the speaker.

Hope blossoms in my chest. My grip tightens round the phone.

'H-hello?' I whisper-shout.

The blossoming hope shrivels at once: there's no response, or at least I don't think it's a response. It's just a random noise or something, so quiet that I wonder if I'm actually hearing it at all, or if the buzzing light over my head is playing tricks on me.

But I press the phone harder to my ear, and then I know I'm not imagining it. It's a strange weird popping sound, pop-pop-pop. And if it was just that, and nothing else, I'd swear it was the phone going odd. Except it's not just that. Because mixed with the popping is something I can't figure out, but whatever it is, it sounds wet. A dull, wet squelching.

Pop. Hiss. Squelch.

Pop. Hiss. Squelch.

Confused, I take the phone from my ear and glance around. 'Hello?' I whisper into the buzzing hallway. 'Someone there?'

No answer.

I put the phone to my ear again.

Pop. Hiss. Squelch.

Pop. Hiss. Squelch.

The pops grow louder. The squelches squelch wetter. Something about them makes me feel icky all over, like when you put your hand in something slimy and gross by accident. It makes me want to follow Mum's second ground rule from a bazillion hours ago and dunk myself in the bath.

Whatever's making the noises, it sounds alive.

The fingers of my left hand twitch, as though searching for the safety of Shoelace's hand . . .

The noises stop.

I whip the phone from my ear. I look at the screen just in time to see it switch itself off.

And that's that.

A million years ago, there used to be house phones, which you'd plug into the wall and every single family on Earth had one, and they didn't need batteries. But this isn't a million years ago, and Shoelace's parents are the last final people who still have one.

My cheeks go hot. Maybe Mum has a secret old house phone stuffed away somewhere? The only places I can think of, though, are her creepy wardrobe room and the cupboard under the stairs, the exact two places I flat-out REFUSE to enter right now.

(Doesn't hurt to check, my deepest-deep-down instincts whisper. Doesn't hurt to check the cupboard under the stairs . . .)

I slip the dead mobile in my rucksack, then glance up the stairs and back down the hallway, searching for anything, anything that could have made those noises, hoping, HOPING they were just in my head.

There's no use lying to myself, though. The noises are already burned into my mind.

Pop. Hiss. Squelch.

I feel the exact same as when I saw the eyes on my phone screen. I know what I heard. I know what I heard, and I know that I didn't imagine it.

Pop. Hiss. Squelch.

The air is sweat-smelling and a trillion degrees, yet my blood is ice.

Pop. Hiss. Squelch.

Pop. Hiss. Squelch.

'K-keep it cool, Lori,' I whisper to myself. 'Shoelace would keep it cool.'

It helps saying Shoelace's name out loud. It makes me stronger.

I can't stay here.

For a horror-studded moment, I honestly consider investigating the cupboard under the stairs for a secret phone. Then I think of the warm breeze, the rattling door, the wrongness in my stomach – and I don't care what my deepest instincts say. I'm staying as far away as humanly actually possible from that awful, horrible cupboard.

That leaves only one other option. At least, one other real option since Mum's wardrobe is a total no-go as well.

Slowly, more slowly than when you sneak up on a spider with a glass in one hand and a sheet of paper in the other, I creep up to the living-room door, and my mind latches on to what Illumamoth-shining-bright wrote all the way back from before I was even born. What twelve-year-old Hazel wrote all the way back, I mean.

That her favourite Voxfriend spoke to her, an illumamoth called Petrie (Pet-tree? Pea-tree? I think you say it Pea-tree). That Petrie-the-illumamoth warned her she was in danger.

Does that mean that Ben could speak to me?

He didn't talk earlier, obviously. Then again, he hasn't been alive very long, so maybe he just didn't realise he could.

I cross every last finger and every last toe, too. If I can talk to my beloved blizzuar, perhaps he can tell me how to escape!

I wrap my fingers round the handle of the living-room door.

'Here goes . . .'

Then I gather my courage and open it.

CHAPTER 21

I do it slowly then creep into the room. The big light is still blown out; the spilled milk has soaked into the carpet like the carpet was thirsty as a spongepottamus in Voxminer, and Voxminer itself is still on the TV. The air is one billion per cent BOILING.

A few hours ago, I would've totally freaked out about the milk. I'd have gone online and watched every video in the literal world about getting rid of stains.

The weird thing is I want that panic. I want my life back: my life of earlier this evening, where the worst thing to worry about was milk on the carpet.

Something new is wrong with Voxminer.

I inch closer to the TV. I was totally ready to find Ben and RoaryCat11 right where I left them, in the weird square hall with the humongously enormous swimming pool in it. However, that's not what I see. Ben and RoaryCat aren't there, and the game's gone back to the start menu.

I think about getting Jonesy from my rucksack to hold him for comfort. It's not just that the game's gone back to the start menu, but that the menu usually shows dozens of different worlds: all the public servers anyone's allowed to join, where you can either battle each other's Voxfriends or work together and stuff, plus all the private ones me and Shoelace created before we started on Kittentopia. We made Fireplace Dave's Magical Land of Chimneys! Detective Mermaid's Giant Bathtub! USS Sisko's Whiskers, which was our attempt to make a one-to-one version of the Monster Kittens' spaceship from Monster Kitten Fighting Force!

All those worlds are gone. The only option left is Kittentopia, except the name is different from what it should be.

It says:

KITTENTOPIA BROOD NEST

Oh, I do not like the sound of that. I don't like it one little bit.

Quickly, before anything else, I open the living-room curtains to make doubly certain there aren't any windows (there aren't because just my luck). Then I squeeze the GG5 controller until my knuckles go white.

I do not, I do NOT want to do this. I HATE this. But I breathe in, breathe out, then select Kittentopia Brood Nest.

The fan whirrs in the GG5.

The world that loads on the screen, however, is not the one me and Shoelace built. It's something that, for whatever reason, I've never tried making in Voxminer before.

My house.

As in my actual house in actual real life, where I'm literally standing right this literally literal second.

I tighten the straps of my rucksack to calm myself. I don't sit down, but stay standing up, and my fingers sweat on the controller.

RoaryCat11 is in Mum's room, in the corner by the bed; if you don't count how cartoony things look, with Voxminer's bright colours and black lines around everything, the room is a perfect copy. The yellow wallpaper is juuust right. The bed is neatly made – just the way it was before I went to sleep and had my nightmare – and the boxes I shoved against the creepy wardrobe room are precisely where they were before.

There aren't any windows in the Voxminer bedroom either, just walls. I think about tunnelling through them. But, when I open my inventory, my heart plummets into my stomach and my stomach into my guts: everything in there, everything, has turned into swamp gunk. That means no shovel. No pickaxe. No sticks of crystal-dynamite that I could've blown up the walls with.

I wipe my forehead. 'It's okay. It's okay, it's okay, it's okay.'

I close the inventory menu, then nudge the joystick a little, and RoaryCat knocks over some boxes, which fall on Mum's carpet. They go thud, thud, thud, though not very loudly.

A horrible thought clanks in my mind. What if I go upstairs and discover the boxes have fallen over in real life? What would that mean?!

I take a deep breath. The air is soul-drainingly hot – GOD, I wish I hadn't broken ground rule number five. And, through the open door of the living room, the frilly light in the downstairs hallway buzzes, and the being-watched feeling grows and grows and grows.

'Shoelace,' I whisper. I know she's not there, but it's nice to pretend she is. 'Shoelace.'

Saying her name gives me just enough strength to ignore the

forever-being-watched feeling – so I make RoaryCat leave Mum's room and head to the Voxminer version of the upstairs landing. Again, it looks so much like it does in real life that my eyes water, and my bedroom is perfect, too. The Voxminer copy of my Monster Kitten alarm clock reads 11:35, the Sea Gang look cuter than ever as cartoons in a video game, and a pair of eyes stare from my bedroom wall at RoaryCat.

'Whoa!'

I make RoaryCat turn to the wall. Whatever was there, though, has already gone. Yet it looked, for a moment, as though a set of wide, watching eyes had formed halfway up the wall beside the bed.

Sharply, I make RoaryCat leave the bedroom, then I open up the Voxfriendopedia.

I'm here for Ben. I am here to speak to Ben. That's all. That's it.

The Voxfriendopedia is empty.

'Oh, you've got to be flipping kidding me,' I mutter. But I check again to be sure, and Ben's 100 per cent definitely not there, and neither are any of my other Voxfriends. The list is empty.

Or, in fact, not totally empty. Not when I look at it properly.

A creeping chill spiders up my back.

Species	L
Nickname (Optional)	O
Biome	R
Level	I

Suitable flesh.

Species	L
Nickname (Optional)	O
Biome	R
Level	I

Suitable mind.

Species	L
Nickname (Optional)	O
Biome	R
Level	I

Suitable flesh.

Species	L
Nickname (Optional)	O
Biome	R
Level	I

Suitable mind.

MORE (Press □)

Frantic, I smash the star button on the GG5 controller, but all the Voxfriend entries are the same.

They're gone. My Voxfriends are gone.

All.

Of.

Them.

Are.

Gone.

My knees shake, but I exit the Voxfriendopedia, then try my best not to collapse on the carpet. At least my Voxfriends haven't been turned into swamp gunk. That's got to be a positive, right?

'Ben's hiding,' I whisper. 'I've just got to find him.'

I make RoaryCat walk down the stairs. She stops under the frilly yellow light in the Voxminer version of the downstairs hallway. And, even though everything else matches up totally perfectly with actual real life, for some reason, the Voxminer version of the living-room door is closed.

My breath goes shallow. Why is the door closed in Voxminer? What's it hiding?

But then another, bigger thought shoves the question from my mind, and my breath gets even quicker: if Voxminer was real, RoaryCat11 would now be standing right outside in the downstairs hallway . . .

RoaryCat, with her black tail and black cat ears that poke from holes in her bright blue beanie.

RoaryCat, sooo cool-looking in her black coat and blue skirt and navy boots.

RoaryCat, who is smart and strong and scared of nothing at all in the whole entire world!

I can't help myself. I twist round and face the real-life doorway again, half expecting to see RoaryCat smiling at me from the hall and giving me a thumbs up. But she's not. There's no one there. The doorframe is completely empty.

'Get a grip, Lori,' I whisper to myself. 'Of course she's not there.'

For now, I don't make RoaryCat enter the Voxminer living room – I think I need to work up to that, build up my nerve a bit more – but, instead, I guide her to the Voxminer kitchen, and find an in-game version of the impossible pinboard where the back door should be. I see my Voxified wellies-with-otters-on-them leaning against the wall.

I see no hint whatsoever of a giant glistening blizzuar.

'Ben. Where are you?!'

I don't actually expect an answer to this. Which is what makes it even more startling when, in the bottom left corner of the TV screen, a message appears:

<Ben_blizzuar> I'm here, Lori. Right behind RoaryCat.

Artwork to come

Where we meet

in the place that binds us

CHAPTER 20

I mustn't hope. I mustn't dare to hope.

But I can't help it. I utterly can't help it. I can't help but hope.

Slowly, I make RoaryCat11 turn round in the Voxminer kitchen.

There sits Ben.

My soul leaps.

It's Ben, it's really Ben, I found him, I FOUND him! He sits neatly in the kitchen doorframe, so gigantic that he takes up almost the whole entire width of it. His two glittering tails swish to and fro. His ears twitch. He fixes icy blue eyes not on RoaryCat11 but, through the TV screen, on me in real life, me clutching the GG5 controller and shivering like a wild thing. Though Voxfriends can't do expressions, little smiling faces appear in the air over his head, which are the symbols that mean a Voxfriend is happy.

Ben stands up. I knew he was big, yet I don't reckon I've ever got before just HOW big. But, seeing him in a video-game version of my house, I can tell that, if he was in real life, he'd be at least as tall as when I stand on tip-toe, or possibly even taller.

He doesn't open his mouth, but text appears in the bottom left-hand corner of the screen, in a slightly see-through box that pops up from nowhere.

Ben's talking to me through the Voxchat feature!

<Ben_blizzuar> Close the door. Your living room is not a place of safety.

There's a ton of colour schemes you can choose for Voxchat, so – naturally – I have it set it to the ocean-biome theme (not like Shoelace who always uses the candy-fields theme). That means the Voxchat box is light blue, Ben's name is purple and his message is seaweed green.

I've never been so relieved to see those special shades of blue, purple and green.

Never.

Weakly, I point behind me at the living-room door. I'm hideously aware of the wasp-buzz of the light in the hallway.

Ben nods.

<Ben_blizzuar> Yes. *That* door.

A claw of sudden doubt jabs me in the belly.

This really is Ben, right? Actually-for-real Ben and not a trick? Could it be Shade Girl in disguise, trying to trap me in the living room?

God, I wish that hadn't just crossed my mind. Yet the thought clings to me like a tac-monkey, aka my least favourite Voxfriend in all existence. I can't peel it off.

I tighten my rucksack again – a ready-to-leg-it type of tightness. Then I gulp and whisper, 'Say something only Ben would know.'

As I speak, writing appears on the TV.

<RoaryCat11> Say something only Ben would know.

I stare at my own words on the screen. Being able to send Voxchat messages without using the in-game keyboard? Sending them just by speaking out loud, without even a microphone or headset? Now, that's something I've not seen in Voxminer before.

Handy, though. Yeah. Pretty flipping handy.

Ben steps from the kitchen doorframe and fully into the actual Voxminer kitchen itself. He rubs himself against RoaryCat, nuzzles her, brushes his massive snowy tails against her – and, I swear, it's like I feel those tails in real life. I can honestly sense his gentleness, his frost-tinged fur. It's the precise exact opposite of the being-watched sensation.

<Ben_blizzuar> You caught me two months, one week, seven hours and sixteen minutes ago.

<Ben_blizzuar> It was in a cave in the Ice Cream Mountains.

<Ben_blizzuar> You told Charlotte you had but a quarter of a heart of health.

<Ben_blizzuar> However, in actuality, you were in

possession of a full heart.

He knows where it happened, and how much health I had. He knows that I'm the only one who's allowed to call Charlie Shoelace, and absolutely no one else on the entire planet of Planet Earth (though thank all Planet Earth that Shoelace isn't here herself to see him call her Charlotte).

And, just like that, I know Ben's 100 per cent who he says he is. A friend.

I rush to the living-room door and shut it – slowly, so it doesn't creak – and, for good measure, I shove one of Mum's big squashy armchairs against it. I have to throw my whole weight into it. Luckily, the chair gives way without making too much noise, then the door is firmly shut.

Without the light from the hallway, the room falls freakishly dark – yet the gloom's not as creepy as I would've thought. Earlier, all I had for company was a stuffed lion doll and the Sea Gang and an imaginary Shoelace. But now I've got Ben. I've got my giant brilliant blizzuar, who can warn me if anything tries sneaking up on me from the shadows.

I hurry back to where I was standing.

<Ben_blizzuar> You should sit down. Allow yourself some rest.

I bite my lower lip. As calm as Ben makes me feel, the thought of sitting in the dark makes me nervous.

I shake my head. 'Sorry. Don't want to.'

Once again, my words appear in the Voxchat box, in the bottom left corner of the TV.

<RoaryCat11> Sorry. Don't want to.

<Ben_blizzuar> You are sure?

<RoaryCat11> Yeah. I'm sure.

Except, suddenly, I'm not so sure. My legs buckle. It's like they're threatening to go on strike unless I sit down right that very utter second.

I didn't realise how worn out I was. I haven't had time to feel worn out. What if I sit down and I'm too tired to get back up again?

<RoaryCat11> Do . . . do you promise it's safe?

<Ben_blizzuar> Apologies but I cannot. You've met with a terrible fate, Lori. Though it is a fate that, even now, at this gravest of stages, has not yet been sealed.

<Ben_blizzuar> Please sit. I shall inform you if you need to run.

It's not the most 100-per-cent-amazing answer, but it's enough that I sit cross-legged on the ruins of my blanket fort. I even take off my Detective Mermaid rucksack, get Jonesy out and plump him on my lap.

<Ben_blizzuar> This way. Hurry.

Ben flicks his tails, heads into the downstairs hallway in Voxminer, and I make RoaryCat11 follow close behind him. It's like their usual positions are reversed.

Then Ben stops by the Voxminer version of my living-room door, which is still shut.

<Ben_blizzuar> In here.

Part of me is properly scared about what I'll find in there. What if – what if I see a Voxminer version of myself, playing Voxminer in Voxminer?!

<Ben_blizzuar> Lori. RoaryCat11 should step into the living room.

<RoaryCat11> H-how come?

<Ben_blizzuar> It is the only room I have succeeded in changing.

<RoaryCat11> I don't get what that means. Does that mean I'm safer in there?

<Ben_blizzuar> No.

<Ben_blizzuar> But it will make you feel better.

<Ben_blizzuar> It is a present. I crafted it especially for you. □

My head throbs. There's sooo much that I just barely, baaarely understand. But I put my trust in Ben, then make RoaryCat11 open the door to the Voxminer living room.

When I see what's inside, I place a slow, quivering hand over my astonished face.

'Oh wow!!' I whisper.

My whisper appears on the screen.

<RoaryCat11> Oh wow!!

CHAPTER 19

Though the rest of the Voxminer house is exactly the same as in real life, the living room is not. It's not even a living room any more.

It's a greenhouse.

Not like the Royal Egg House in Kittentopia, but a greenhouse that must be the single most incredible creation I've ever seen in all entire Voxminer!

My mouth drops open as I move RoaryCat11 inside. Ben follows. The door shuts by itself behind him.

The greenhouse is smallish, only about twice the size of Mum's room. Yet it doesn't feel small because a gazillion stars glitter through the windows in a deep navy sky, and plants and flowers line the walls, and they're all different colours. The floor glistens with ruby and emerald, diamond and sapphire, and in the middle of the crystal tiled floor is a heart-shaped pond. A fountain shoots up from the pond. It reaches the domed ceiling, then falls back down with a soft splashing sound.

Everything's lit by dozens of lights scattered over the tiles like fallen stars – not moonglow-lanterns, but, instead, they're shaped like flowers of delicate sparkle-glass, all blue and pink and purple and stuff.

None of them buzz.

A smile tugs at my mouth. The lights don't buzz. Thank God, they make no sound whatsoever!

But it's not just glass-spun flowers that glow: the frame of the greenhouse is made completely from heart-star, a type of Voxminer crystal so rare that me and Shoelace have never even found any before. The most we've ever seen is when VoxFox64 spent a whole week streaming his adventures searching in the night sky for it, building castles from freshly mined cloudium and herding zoxens. Even then, he found less than a dozen Voxblocks worth.

I shake from wonder. The heart-star is silvery. Sparkling strains of pale blue light gently pulse through it.

A figure lurks in the corner, framed against the light.

My breath catches! Before I even know what's happening, the figure rushes up to RoaryCat. My heart bursts with terror—

<Shoelace> ROARS!!!!!!!!!!!!!!!!!!

The very utter instant I see Shoelace's name in the Voxchat box, my fear flips on its head, transforms into joy.

'SHOELACE!!!!!'

<RoaryCat11> SHOELACE!!!!!

I clasp a hand over my mouth. I glance at the living-room door and at the big old armchair shoved up against it: luckily, I don't hear anything stir in the downstairs hallway. All I can do is hope it stays that way, and pray that nothing heard me yell Shoelace's name.

Shush! I tell myself off in my head.

Quivering quietly – quietly – I give Jonesy a quick little squeeze, then turn back to the TV.

Shoelace has already left some new messages.

<Shoelace> Where are you??????????????????

<Shoelace> Everyone looking for you!!!!!!!!!!

I don't answer. I just stare at her, stare at Shoelace's player character, with her dark hair, dark skin, pointy fox ears, her bright red wizard's robe with pink and purple stars on it, and the big fluffy fox tail that pokes from her back.

When I look at her, I don't even see a character in Voxminer. All I see is Shoelace. All I see is Charlie, as real as though she's not on the TV, but in the actual literal living room with me.

I sob. I can't hold it back. Tears gush down my cheeks, and I sob and I sob and I sob.

Shoelace found me. She actually really found me.

She's HERE.

<Shoelace> Roars speak to me

<Shoelace> you okay??

<Shoelace> where you at?!?!?!?!?

Shoelace can't keep still. She runs round the little greenhouse, though doesn't take her eyes from RoaryCat11. Unlike Ben, I guess she can't see me in real life through the TV screen. I think she can only see what appears in Voxminer . . .

I force down my sobs, whisper out loud, and my words appear in the Voxchat box.

<RoaryCat11> I don't . . . I don't . . .

<RoaryCat11> God, Shoelace, I don't even know

<RoaryCat11> I'm in my house, but it's weird

<RoaryCat11> All the doors and windows are gone, I can't get out

<Shoelace> wait roars your in your house??

<Shoelace> your mum already looked there tho

My fingers clench round the GG5 controller. Mum's been home? When??

<RoaryCat11> I'm scared

<RoaryCat11> Shoelace, I'm so scared I'm scared I'm so so scared

<Shoelace> Roars it okay

<Shoelace> wherever you are im gonna get you out

<Shoelace> also sorry this sound dumb but

<Shoelace> . . . . . .

A little message that says Shoelace is typing appears then

disappears over and over in the Voxchat box. It's like she keeps deleting messages without sending them.

I cock my head. It's totally unShoelacey not to be 100 per cent forward 100 per cent of the time. What's she writing that she keeps second-guessing?

Eventually, she asks a question, and it's short.

It stabs.

<Shoelace> are you in Voxminer????!!!!

I stare at the strange words on the screen.

Am I in Voxminer?

I don't . . . think so? The living room certainly doesn't look like it's in a video game, plus I'm playing Voxminer right this instant on the TV!

But I don't even answer since Shoelace's messages start coming ultra-fast, and there are spelling mistakes in every single one of them.

<Shoelace> sorry dum bquestion its just

<Shoelace> g ot bck from aunts party

<Shoelace> then your mum ringour house

<Shoelace> you missig

<Shoelace> no one know where yo ar

<Shoelace> your mum keep phoing in case you come to mine

<Shoelace> i go on vM Since you said earlier you

playng it

<Shoelace> maybe i fnd clue??

Dread wraps round me as I read Shoelace's story. I see it happen in my mind. I hear it happen. It's waaay too easy to imagine Mum's desperate voice as she phones Shoelace's parents and explains that I'm missing.

It's what Shoelace types next, though, that sends my heart into absolute overdrive.

<Shoelace> when I open VM, KIttentopia difernet

<Shoelace> its called kittetopia broom nest???!??!?!

<Shoelace> also it not Kittentopia. its just your house but strange???

<Shoelace> no dorrs windows. goes up down frever

<Shoelace> also i find ben and he speak now?? tell me to wait in grenehouse???

<Shoelace> ALSO also I try show my mum but she can't see what I see???????$WEF?D

<Shoelace> all mum dad see is normal Kittentopia???!??!??????????????????????????

I sit up straighter. Jonesy flops on my lap. It's not just me Kittentopia's changed for, then, but Shoelace as well. She can see the changes, too!

Yet, for some reason, her parents can't.

How does that make any sense? How can Shoelace's mum see something different from Shoelace? And what does 'goes up down frever' mean? What goes up and down forever?!

'Wh-what d'you mean?' I ask.

<RoaryCat11> Wh-what d'you mean?

<Shoelace> I mean no one believe what im saying

<RoaryCat11> Can't your mum see my house?!

<Shoelace> all anyone else see is normal vm, mum think I'm near mount tuna paste mountainb. She say stop being silly chalie

My heart beats fast-fast-fast-fast. I don't understand. I don't understand.

Ben slinks by Shoelace's side. He swishes his tails and says:

<Ben_blizzuar> You two are the only ones who can see the changes. No one else.

<Ben_blizzuar> Because this is YOUR world, the world you built together. You understand it in ways that others simply cannot. You perceive the truth of it, the truth others cannot see.

<Ben_blizzuar> This world BINDS you.

I don't even respond, but something in what he says makes me feel closer to Shoelace than I've ever felt in my entire total life.

Shoelace shuffles on the screen.

<Shoelace> . . . . . . am I right tho??

<Shoelace> Roars does this mean you really in VM?????

Hot, stuffy air presses round my body.

<RoaryCat11> Honest to God, I don't know where I am.

<RoaryCat11> I don't think it's Voxminer though. I'm starting to think it's not OUR world either. I think I'm somewhere else.

<RoaryCat11> I tried yelling for my neighbours. No one heard me.

<RoaryCat11> What if it's cos they're not even there?

The thought slivers into my head, a cold, wretched little thing. Perhaps the reason my neighbours didn't hear me is because they aren't there. Perhaps the whole world isn't there. If I could peek outside my house, maybe all I'd find is black endlessness, like when you use the death-clipping glitch to glitch past the absolute edge of your Voxminer world, and then you end up in a weird blank nothingness where nothing loads properly, nothing whatsoever.

Voxminer fans call it the Blockless Abyss. Or the Abyss for short.

Is that where I am? Is my house floating in the Blockless Abyss?!

Shoelace doesn't give me time to freak out.

<Shoelace> I believe you

And there they are: the three golden words I didn't know I needed to see.

Tears stream down my face all of a sudden, and my nose clogs, and my cheeks burn up. One friend in a million would believe me about all this. One in ten million.

That friend is Shoelace.

Thank God, thank utter total God for Shoelace.

And thank God for Ben as well! Because the massive blizzuar steps between RoaryCat11 and Shoelace and says:

<Ben_blizzuar> My apologies. I wish not to interrupt.

<Ben_blizzuar> There is much that requires explanation, yet your time is almost up. But we are here to help you, Lori.

<Ben_blizzuar> Help you escape.

CHAPTER 18

<RoaryCat11> What do I do, Ben?

<RoaryCat11> Where even am I? Is this the Abyss?

<RoaryCat11> Also, is it Shade Girl? Is Shade Girl the one who's after me?

<RoaryCat11> What does she even want with me?!

I only mean to ask the first question, but the others pour from me. Shoelace jumps up and down on the screen.

<Shoelace> WAIT SHADE GIRLS AFTER YO?!?!?!/111

'Shush!!!' I hiss at her.

<RoaryCat11> Shush!!!

A wisp of embarrassment coils round my stomach. No one can hear Shoelace shouting in all-caps. I'm – I'm being jumpy.

<RoaryCat11> Wait, sorry. Why did I say that?

<RoaryCat11> Sorry

<Shoelace> lol

I roll my eyes but grin. Trust Shoelace to toss in a lol at a time like this.

Ben paces back and forth on his icy, sparkling paws.

<Ben_blizzuar> Why does Shade Girl desire you?

<Ben_blizzuar> Therein lies the mystery. She is old, Lori, older than Voxminer, older than any living being. In that ocean of centuries, endless shadows she has woven across her heart.

<Ben_blizzuar> I cannot pierce the veil of her intentions.

<Ben_blizzuar> All I truly know of her is that she is responsible for my existence.

I goggle at the screen. It's not just the way Ben talks (do all Voxfriends sound like they were taught how to speak by strange old wizards??), but what he's saying is so much to take in.

Judging from what Shoelace types, I reckon she's goggling, too.

<Shoelace> SHUT UP NO WAY

<Shoelace> she brought ou to life?!?

Smiling little faces appear over Ben's head.

<Ben_blizzuar> Not on purpose.

<Ben_blizzuar> I believe she is unaware of me. Yet, over the years, such infinities of magic have crystallised round her that oddities are bound to occur.

'Oddities?' I ask. 'You mean like you?'

Ben nods. The happy faces vanish.

<Ben_blizzuar> Correct. Oddities such as I.

<Ben_blizzuar> To address your other questions: you are not in Voxminer.

<Ben_blizzuar> But neither are you in real life.

<Ben_blizzuar> You are somewhere else. A third place. Somewhere outside the boundaries of both your living, breathing world and the world of Voxminer.

My heart pounds.

<RoaryCat11> How do you know?

<Ben_blizzuar> I feel snatches of Shade Girl's thoughts.

<Ben_blizzuar> I believe it to be a side effect of her magic granting me life. I believe her magic makes us connected.

Shoelace jumps around again, impatient.

<Shoelace> never mind that

<Shoelace> how Lori escape????

Ben sits neatly on the crystal floor.

<Ben_blizzuar> Lori must use her power.

It's yet another thing I don't know how to respond to. My power? Shoelace types faster than I can even speak.

<Shoelace> lol you saying Roars is witch?

Ben flicks his tails. Both of them.

<Ben_blizzuar> No, Charlotte.

<Shoelace> CHARLIE!!!

<Shoelace> MY NAME SCHARLIE NOT CHARLOTE!!!!

<Shoelace> GET IT RIGHT!!!!¬~£!£R!

<Shoelace> ....

<Shoelace> sorry

<Shoelace> that rude of me ☐

Ben bows his head. He answers in a way that, if it was anyone else on Earth, I'd swear they were being sarcastic. Yet Ben's not on Earth. He's in Voxminer. And, coming from him, it doesn't feel sarcastic at all.

<Ben_blizzuar> My sincerest apologies – Charlie.

<Ben_blizzuar> I mean that Lori is in a place where she has power. Magic.

I huff.

<RoaryCat11> WHAT magic? I don't have magic, do I??

<Ben_blizzuar> You have love.

<Ben_blizzuar> Your heart blazes with love.

<Ben_blizzuar> In the place where you are trapped, love is magic. Love is power.

It sounds like something from a Shimmer Squad novel, or something the Atomic Slacker would say, aka the leader of Monster Kitten Fighting Force. Yet, coming from a giant blizzuar with glistening fur and eyes that are all wise and serious, the words feel so powerful that I don't even question them.

Love is magic.

Love is power.

A shiver starts from the tips of my toes and travels all the way to the top of my head. I don't know precisely what love is power means. But, in my heart, I know that it's the truth. The sincere, total, absolute truth.

<Ben_blizzuar> Close your eyes, Lori.

<Ben_blizzuar> Focus upon your heart.

<Ben_blizzuar> Do you feel it?

The living room is dark, the being-watched feeling is strong, and so I don't shut my eyes. Instead, I take a deep breath and focus on my heart as best I can.

Shoelace races around on the screen.

<Shoelace> this is dumb!!!

<Shoelace> Ben just say where Roars needs to go!!!!!!

Then I gasp.

'No, no!' I hiss at Shoelace. Her player character stops in her tracks. 'Ben's right. I can feel something.'

And I can.

It's another tug on my heart – the tiniest, most littlest tiny tug in the entire world. It's so small that, without Ben's help, I would never in a hundred actual years have ever noticed it. Yet, in the same way that some weird, invisible force led me through Shade Girl's labyrinth of swimming pools, this new tug-on-my-heart tells me where I need to go.

The difference, this time, is that it's a nice feeling. The tug is warm. Gentle.

It says to head–

<RoaryCat11> Wait, wait.

<RoaryCat11> Ben, this can't be right, can it?

<RoaryCat11> I need to go downwards??

The tug insists that the way to escape is to go down, down, so impossibly, wildly far down that my stomach turns twisty. I don't get it. I don't understand at all. My house doesn't even have a basement!

Yet it has a cupboard under the stairs: it has a cupboard under the stairs, and there was a weird warm breeze coming from it. And I think I finally get why my deepest most deep, deep instincts whispered that possibly, perhaps, and maybe, just maybe, exploring the cupboard wouldn't be the worst idea in the universe . . .

I seize up. Jonesy falls from my lap on to the carpet, but I'm frozen all of a sudden, so I don't pick him up again.

The cupboard under the stairs can't be the answer. It CAN'T be. There's nothing in there except a broom and a mop and a battered old hoover!

But Ben looks at me through the screen and says:

<Ben_blizzuar> There is a spot in Shade Girl's nest. It is a place where centuries of excess magic has built up, like dust that gathers in a forgotten corner.

<Ben_blizzuar> The magic has caused the barrier between her world and yours to wear thin.

<Ben_blizzuar> If you can find the place where the barrier has worn thin, you can break it. You can tear a hole in it simply by yearning for it. You can return to where you belong.

I wanted answers, yet the answers make me more confused than ever. But I think I get the absolute basics.

I need to follow the tug that pulls on my heart. I need to do it fast, since time's running out and Shade Girl could appear at any literal second.

If I follow the tug – if I trust in it, trust in Ben's words, trust that investigating the cupboard under the stairs isn't the most breathlessly awful idea any girl's ever come up with – then the tug will guide me to a spot where I can escape back home. My real home, where Mum and Shoelace wait for me.

I gulp. I do NOT want to open the cupboard under the stairs, the cupboard that feels so wrong, wrong, wrong, wrong—

'What about Shade Girl?' I whisper. 'What if she gets me before I escape?'

<Ben_blizzuar> Remember what I said.

<Ben_blizzuar> Love is power.

<Ben_blizzuar> Love is deadly to her.

It's all well and good saying love is power, but what does that actually mean? If Shade Girl attacks me, do I give her a sweet little hug? A kiss on the forehead? Call me raving, but something tells me Shade Girl wouldn't appreciate a lovely warm kiss slap in the middle of her forehead.

Suddenly Ben goes tense. His tails straighten. Red exclamation marks appear over his head.

Shoelace types something, and her messages send lightning though my bones.

<Shoelace> Roars??

<Shoelace> roars somethings happieng

<Shoelace> my screen going funny

I'm on my feet, I'm shaking, and I don't need to ask what's happening to Shoelace's laptop since I reckon it's the same thing happening to the TV.

The screen flickers. Flashes of static race across it, then cover it completely.

I've seen something like this before, in a lesson last year when Ms Newt brought in an olden-times TV from when she was our age. It was small, but also weirdly chunky, and made from silver plastic and shaped like a moonglow-lantern.

Ms Newt plugged it in at the front of the class, and the screen filled with a million white and black dots that danced around totally at random. A weird noise came from the speakers. It was like waves at the seaside, but all distorted and speeded up.

'Ms,' Shoelace cooed from near the back of the class, 'I don't think your TV is feeling well. I think it's poorly, Ms.'

Ms Newt smiled at her. 'Actually, Charlie, what you're seeing right now is cosmic radiation. Space, children. What you can see on the screen comes from deepest, darkest, coldest space!'

She explained how, when they're not switched to any particular channel, old TVs pick up ancient signals from outer space. That means radiation shot out by exploding stars. It means energy spat out from black holes from a million-times-a-zillion miles away, and it even means stuff from the Big Bang from actual billions of years ago!

To be honest, I didn't quite get it. I STILL don't get it. It felt so mysterious, kind of eerie even. As though the TV was showing us ghosts from all the way back from the Beginning of Time . . .

Whatever the living-room TV is picking up now, it's probably not radiation from outer space. It's something closer, but just as mysterious and a gazillion times freakier.

The static clears up for a second, just enough for me to see Shoelace's player character panicking round the greenhouse, and Ben in his attack position, ready for action, ice spreading over the tiles round his paws.

He says:

<Ben_blizzuar> Lori

<Ben_blizzuar> RUN

The static comes back, but I don't wait around. I drop the GG5 controller, grab Jonesy, shoot to my feet—

Then I freeze at once, since the being-watched feeling suddenly grows so massive that my insides shrivel behind my ribs.

There's a squelching noise. It comes from all around. From the walls. The sofa. The ceiling.

Dreading – God, DREADING – what I am about to see, I hug Jonesy. Breathe in as deep as I utterly can. Straighten up. Look round the living room.

And

eyes

stare

back

at

me.

<insert artwork – galaxy of eyes>

Artwork to come

CHAPTER 17

They are the eyes from my nightmare, the eyes from Mum's mattress, except they're not fabric this time, but real. They glare from where they've sprouted over the walls and ceiling, and on the sofa, too, and they glisten wetly in the static. Most are normal-sized, though some are as small and beady as the eyes of dark creatures in the lurking night. Others are as big as my palm, big as my face, and a handful are even larger than that. And the eyes form patterns of curls and swirls and spirals – living, watching, wetly gleaming galaxies.

They don't blink. All of them stay wide, wide open.

I drop Jonesy again – clap my hands over my mouth – stagger backwards—

The galaxies of eyes follow me. Only the floor remains eyeless, and the corner where the door to the hallway is.

I bump into the TV, almost knock it from the stand. Every bone and muscle screams at me that I'm in danger, the MOST danger.

But I can't move, I can't move, I'm too petrified to move. The most I can do is look at the static on the TV. It clears up again, just enough to make out Voxminer.

<Shoelace> LORI LORI

<Shoelace> SAY WAHTS HAPPENING WHATS HAPOPEBNING?!/1/1/1

<Shoelace> WHATS HAPEPNING?!:!¬~~£>1,2RBJH

The static gets denser. Voxminer vanishes again.

In blood-pounding silence, the eyes all swivel to the living-room door.

The door rattles.

'M-Mum,' I breathe. 'Ben. Shoelace. Help . . .'

Whatever's on the other side of the door, it doesn't make much effort to try and push the armchair back. Isn't it strong enough? Or perhaps it is strong enough, and it's taunting me.

Either way, whatever is coming for me, it's hungry. Whatever is in the downstairs hallway, it's evil. Oh Lord, I'm pummelled with such a sense of downright evil that it's like my heart is being crushed, like I'm pinned under the utter freezing weight of it.

More eyes sprout over the walls and gaze at the door. Then I gape as finally, at last, the thing in the hallway forces its way through.

The door doesn't open much: just enough to shove back the armchair a few centimetres. It's enough, though, and it's as if there's suddenly nothing between me and it, nothing to hide or cower behind.

I hear a voice.

It is the worst voice. It's deep, deep, and wet, wet, like whatever's speaking is underwater, or as if their mouth swims with swamp gunk. If it was saying anything else at all, I don't reckon I'd understand it.

But it says the literal most terrible thing imaginable.

LORI . . .

Vomit-swirlingly slowly, long thin fingers, fingers the length of one of my arms, appear through the gap and wrap round the door – fingers like the legs of a gigantic spider.

They're sickly white and grope about, jerky, twitchy. They have too many joints. They don't have claws or nails, but each of her five fingers get thinner and thinner towards the tips, and end in vicious-looking points that scratch against the wood.

Scratch.

Scratch.

LORI . . .

There's no doubting it: those fingers belong to Shade Girl.

They're followed by a pale, terrible arm. She pokes it through the gap, bone-thin and waaay too long. Oh gosh, why won't the arm stop coming?!

Scratch.

Scratch.

Squelch.

Squelch.

For a moment, I think it's the eyes that squelch, but it's not. They still don't blink. Something else is making that sound.

Squelch.

Squelch.

I've heard it before.

Pop. Hiss. Squelch.

I heard it on my phone. Back on the staircase, before my phone went dead.

Pop. Hiss. Squelch.

A second arm appears. Nightmare fingers stab into the armchair, then the arms start to pull. With all her might, Shade Girl tries to squeeze the rest of her body through the tiny gap in the door.

Her stink slams into me; I almost crumple to my knees. It's the stench of curdled milk soaking into the living-room carpet, of mould-eaten fruit left in the sun and coated in flies. It's so pungent that I don't just smell it, but fully taste it on my tongue.

Then Shade Girl's body squelches into view and, lit only by the dancing static from the TV, she's tricky to properly make sense of. But she's dark and wet-looking and kind of see-through, like jelly, yet jelly if it was made from shadows and midnight. Her body glistens in the static. She is soaking.

LORI . . .

More of Shade Girl's wet, lumpy body appears, and the lumps go slop-slop-slop as they squeeze through the tiny gap. Her body is formed from balls of jelly, all glooped together! In the dark centre of each slimy ball, I spy a tiny orb of pale white floating in mucus. I don't know what they are, but the orbs are diseased-looking. They make my skin creep.

The door creaks further open, then the rest of Shade Girl pours into the living room. She sloshes on to the armchair.

I scream, SCREAM. Because, now she's in front of me, I understand what I'm seeing.

The armchair groans because Shade Girl is huge; she's GIANT; she's twice as big as a grown-up. Her body's made from hundreds of eggs squashed together in a gooey cluster – not the bright rainbow eggs that hatch into Voxfriends, or even the weird black ones me and Ben found at the end of the swimming-pool maze. Instead, they're like frogspawn, except each of the eggs is the size of my head. Stabbing from the nightmare of eggs are Shade Girl's thin, terrible arms with their long spidery fingers. I spot her legs. They're tiny, like two scribbles of white, as if they don't have any bones, but are made from dead meat. They drag uselessly behind the mass of her egg-sac body.

Shade Girl doesn't have a head. She's a giant of slime and arms and legs and eggs.

Do the eyes belong to her as well, the eyes on the walls, the ceiling and the sofa? Is that how she sees?!

Also, just because I can't make out a face, there must be a mouth somewhere beneath those eggs, or how could she say my name? Plus I can hear her breathing. It's like when Mum got ultra-ill one time and had to fight for every last breath. The doctors said her lungs were full of fluid. You could hear it. You could actually for real hear it. Her breath spluttered. It sounded wet.

Shade Girl's rasping is even wetter. Every breath is a battle and skull-crunchingly loud. God, it's loud. It makes my own lungs hurt. Makes me feel like I'm drowning.

The eyes on the walls turn back towards me – then Shade Girl slops heavily on to the carpet. The floorboards shake. She raises her arms almost all the way to the ceiling, then brings them down and drags herself over the floor.

My eyes water from Shade Girl's stench—

I scream again—

Stumble, fall, scramble backwards against the nearest wall, which is moist with eyes – my pyjamas drip with sweat—

Slime trails behind Shade Girl. Her egg-sac body wobbles. It hisses – I think it's the sound of air being forced between her eggs – and I hear dreadful noises like popping water balloons, as though smaller hidden eggs are being squashed deep inside her like bubble wrap. Some of her looser eggs drop off and splat on the floor.

She reaches out to me, her breath gasping, wheezing—

'GET AWAY FROM ME!'

Shade Girl doesn't listen. She raises her sharp, horrible fingers in the air, makes a deep-throated growl that rattles my bones—

'GET AWAY!'

I'm trapped. I can't run.

'GET AWAY!!'

Driblets of slime ooze from between Shade Girl's eggs. She brings her fingers down right on top of me—

I scrunch up against the wall of eyes – their wetness soaks into my pyjamas. My ears ring and I'm screaming, screaming, screaming—

Scratch.

CHAPTER 16

One of the spidery razor tips of Shade Girl's fingers tears my pyjama bottoms, slices my left leg like my skin is paper. White fire erupts through my shin. Red mist explodes in my vision. I clutch my leg. I HOWL.

My palms turn wet, and the wetness is warm.

I don't look at my hands. I don't dare look at them.

I stare at Shade Girl.

Shade Girl gives a deep, guttural growl.

She drags herself closer. Towers. Raises an arm again.

Mum's face flashes in my mind and Shoelace's, too.

Crazily, I remember Shoelace's smile. I scrunch my eyes as much as I can, so that Shoelace's smile is the last thing I'll ever, ever see.

Just as I do . . .

Something happens.

Even with my eyes tight shut, my vision fills with whiteness – and, for an insane moment, I realise that I'm dead, and that dying didn't hurt, and that I'm dead and that I'm dead and that I'm dead.

Except I can't be dead. My leg still kills from where Shade Girl got me. If I was dead, wouldn't the pain just stop?

The whiteness grows brighter.

Shade Girl splutters.

I take a terrified breath, force my eyes back open – and gasp.

It's the TV! The screen shines so bright that I throw a warm, wet hand over my face and watch through my fingers!

Shade Girl backs away from the light. The bazillion eyes on the walls and furniture wince and squint. They turn filmy. Blind-looking.

Then they shut their eyelids and vanish.

My heart gallops. One by one, then dozen by dozen, then hundred by hundred, the eyes literally wink from existence, and then they are gone. Shade Girl flails in the middle of the living room, like she can't see where she is any more.

But I turn from Shade Girl back to the TV, because a golden, glowing tendril emerges from the screen and weaves through the air like a ribbon. The ribbon is the length of my body, yet only the width of my thumbs. It's made from absolute pure light.

The golden ribbon wraps round the gash on my leg, and it's cold, oh gosh, the ribbon is wonderfully, beautifully, amazingly cold against the inferno of my wound. My eyes tear up from how INCREDIBLE it feels.

Then the ribbon unwinds itself from me, and the pain is gone.

I glance at my leg. There's no blood. There's none soaked into my pyjama bottoms and there's none on my palms either, even though the ribbon never even touched them. All that's left is an angry white scar that reaches from my knee to my foot. My belly swirls from looking at it.

The ribbon dances goldingly through the air above Shade Girl. It circles her, and Shade Girl stops flailing and cowers instead.

The ribbon grows. It gets longer and longer.

Then I hear a voice.

Ben's voice.

I haven't heard him speak out loud before, yet I know that it's him. It's as deep as a jaguar's, as strong as a million lions all roaring at the exact same second.

'**Lori Alex Mills**,' he says. '**I love you.**'

My soul sings.

And when he says that he loves me I feel it. I actually for real feel it. It's a song in my blood. A chorus beneath my skin.

His love feeds me energy. Enough energy that I force myself to my feet.

Then the ribbon twirls close to the floor and wraps itself round Jonesy, who is still lying by the GG5 controller.

'Jonesy!' I gasp.

Ben's voice comes from nowhere again. Or from everywhere. I don't know which.

'**I can hold Shade Girl off for a few seconds more. But you will need to leave Jonesy behind.**'

The song in my blood dies. 'But—'

'**Jonesy is imbued with love. He is the only object strong enough to contain my essence.**'

Sudden tears waterfall down my face. I don't understand. I don't want to leave Jonesy. I can't leave him. Getting him is almost the first thing I can remember – a present from Mum on my third birthday. He's my FRIEND.

But if I stay here I'll die . . .

I swallow. Wipe my eyes. If Ben says he needs Jonesy, then he needs him, even if I don't get why. And if Jonesy could talk he would tell me to trust in Ben.

'Wh-where do I go?' I splutter.

I already know. Ben already told me. Yet I hope against hope he'll give a different answer this time.

He doesn't.

'**Down. Follow the tug – the tug-on-your-heart. Trust in it, even when the way turns dark, and the darkness eclipses the light of hope. Keep going. Keep going. Keep going.**' He pauses, then adds, '**Goodbye, Lori Mills. It was an honour being your blizzuar.**'

I don't know how to respond, so I just gulp and whisper, 'I love you, too.'

Shade Girl still cowers from the light of the ribbon. She coils her terrible arms round her humongous egg-sac body.

Then the ribbon of light sinks into Jonesy, sinks inside his little lion body so that he shines from within and goes utterly blazingly golden. He's bright as a star.

Shade Girl SHRIEKS.

With a longing glance at Jonesy, my Jonesy, my treasure, I run. I rush past the desperately quaking Shade Girl, grab my rucksack, sling it on, then take hold of the armchair against the door and pull with all my heart and soul and muscles. It's *sooo* heavy.

'MOVE!' I scream at it.

The chair gives way and lurches over the carpet. The living-room door swings open.

Jonesy EXPLODES.

I shoot one last final glance at him – just in time to watch him blow up in a flash of the brightest most blinding light in the absolute world.

Shade Girl wails. She shrivels against the wall, stunned, frozen in place.

'JONESY!' I screech. **'BEN!'**

But I feel the truth, the truth in my heart: they're gone. Both of them. Ben must have done something with his magic – pushed himself beyond his limits.

Whatever he did, he gave himself up to save me. To give me a chance, just the teeniest, tiniest, most littlest little chance of all.

I won't let it be for nothing. I WON'T.

So I don't cry, but throw myself into the downstairs hallway before Shade Girl can recover and slam the living-room door behind me.

CHAPTER 15

I'm in the kitchen in less than a second, yet halt before the cupboard under the stairs.

The strange breeze is stronger: it's warmer; it's boiling. The cupboard door shakes – and what will I find when I open it? What if it's something bad? Something even worse than Shade Girl?!

Sweat streams down my face.

'T-trust in the tug,' I whisper. 'Trust in it. Open the door, just open it, open it—'

I hear a roar, followed by a SMACK. I think Shade Girl's throwing all her might against the living-room door.

I've waited too long: barely seconds, yet every single one of those seconds is treasure-hoard precious. So I trust in the tug, trust in it, trust in it – then wrap my fingers round the handle and open the battered brown door.

The inside of the cupboard has vanished.

So has the broom, the mop and the hoover, and the cobwebs that called the cupboard home. Instead, a musty staircase tumbles down and down, low, steep and thin. The steps, walls and ceiling are made from filthy, damp-smelling wood. A grotty yellow lightbulb dangles from the ceiling halfway down the stairs on a frayed wire. The bulb flickers. It buzzes, and the buzz is stark and super ultra-threatening.

The air is scorching. Tight. Suffocating. It's a tiger-staircase: every instinct warns me to stay still and not set foot on the impossible steps.

Almost every instinct.

'Run,' says the tug-on-my-heart. 'RUN.'

I groan and TEAR down the staircase, take the steps three at a time. But the wood is soft and rotten, and it crumbles under my feet. I scream, throw out my hands, but I can't slow down—

I smash into a wall at the bottom of the stairs. I don't pause, but turn to the left, where light spills from a white wooden door, slightly open. I hurl myself through it, then halt once again.

Confusion holds me in place, along with dark wonder and sheer, utter terror. I didn't know where the stairs would lead. Yet not once in a gazillion years did I think they'd lead to—

'Mum's room?!'

Because that's when I realise I've just thrown myself out of Mum's weird, creepy wardrobe room.

Mum's wallpaper is its normal yellow. The curtains are open; the windows are still gone. The only thing different are her boxes and folders, which should've been stacked against the wardrobe door that I've just burst through. Instead, they're strewn across the carpet.

This can't be right. It completely and categorically can't be right. The tug-on-my-heart promised I was heading downwards. So how can I be upstairs again? Was there something I was meant to do that Ben forgot to tell me about?!

'Keep going,' I imagine Ben saying. 'Keep going. Keep going.'

Despite Ben's words, I poke my head back through the wardrobe door and glance around to make sure I didn't miss something.

Then horror floods my absolute bloodstream because I see her.

Shade Girl.

The towering nightmare mass of her fills the doorframe at the top of the decaying wooden steps – fills it completely. Her body glistens in the filthy yellow light. Her arms are long and terrible, her fingers sharp, her stench retch-worthy.

She roars an otherworldly roar, then THROWS herself down the stairs, right towards me—

I don't even close the wardrobe door: I just run – faster than any girl ever in history – fly through the open door of Mum's room and across the landing and down the regular stairs to the hallway—

I

don’t

stop

running

running

down

down

down.

CHAPTER 14

I'm back in the kitchen. The cupboard under the stairs is shut again.

There's barely time to register it. Shade Girl didn't close the door behind her – she can't have done, not unless she ran back up the stairs for some reason. So how can it be shut? Did it close by itself?

I don't stop to think. I open the cupboard again, and once more the impossible staircase greets me with its low ceiling and dank-smelling steps.

Shade Girl roars my name from somewhere behind me. <text-shadegirl> LORI! </text-shadegirl> she screams—

I pretty much JUMP down the stairs—

Hurry through the door at the bottom again—

Once again, I'm in Mum's room.

It's totally impossible, yet here I am. I'm in Mum's room. Mum's room. The bed is unmade. The windows are gone. Boxes are scattered across the floor.

HOW am I in Mum's room? How's it possible to head downstairs yet end up upstairs?!

On a hunch, I grab Mum's duvet from where it hangs halfway off the bed, and throw it fully on the floor—

I race to the downstairs hallway—

Back to the kitchen—

For the third time, the cupboard under the stairs is shut. It should be wide, wide open, and yet it's shut.

For the third time, I yank it open.

For the third time, I rush down the impossible staircase.

And, for the third time, I'm in Mum's room – but this time, this time, I'm prepared for it. So, even though I don't stop sprinting, I spot at once what I'm searching for: Mum's duvet. It's not where I hurled it on the floor. No, it's gone right back to where it started, in an identical messy heap hanging half over the edge of the bed.

In the corners of my mind, I start to grasp what's happening.

This isn't my normal house. It's – it's just a photocopy of it or something: a near-perfect version of what it looked like when I woke up screaming from my nightmare earlier that night. Every time I open the cupboard under the stairs and dash down the impossible steps, I find myself in yet another copy, then another, then another, another, another, another. Copies of my house all the way down.

My soul sinks. How many copies are there? Is there even an end to them?!

LORI! Shade Girl booms.

I don't know how far behind she is, but she's close, waaay too close.

LORI!

I rush down the regular staircase—

Race into the kitchen, through the cupboard door, then down the fourth identical set of impossible stairs—

Into Mum's room, down the landing again, down the regular staircase—

Down the fifth impossible staircase—

The fifth version of Mum's room—

The landing—

Regular stairs—

Kitchen—

Impossible stairs—

Mum's room—

Regular stairs—

Kitchen—

Impossible stairs—

My bones are on fire, but I run even faster, and Shade Girl's roars get further away. I think she's two, perhaps three, copies of my house behind me by now.

The copies begin to change.

House by house, the air gets hotter, wetter and the carpets grow damper. I think of warm, soggy places deep in the Earth, perfect for moist creatures to build their nests in. I think of basements. I think of walls closing in, of tunnels and caves getting smaller and smaller the deeper you go.

A few copies of my house further down, the air gets so waterlogged that, everywhere I look, the yellowish-cream wallpaper peels, and the plaster behind it is coated in mould. Water starts pooling on all the different landings. It splashes down the stairs in trickling streams – down both sets of stairs, the regular ones and the impossible ones. The air gets so thick that my breath mists, and it's like trying to breathe soup.

Yet even now I don't slow down. Shade Girl's far enough behind that I can barely hear her, but

I

do

NOT.

SLOW.

DOWN.

CHAPTER 13

<insert map of room 1>

CHAPTER 12

<insert map of room 2>

CHAPTER 11

d

o

w

n

CHAPTER 10

d

o

w

n

CHAPTER
9

d

o

w

n

I stop.

Artwork to come

Where you guide me through

water and starlight

CHAPTER 8

I'm on yet another landing, just outside my bedroom at the top of what must be the billionth copy of the regular staircase. Yet there's nowhere to go since this version of my house isn't like all the rest. For starters, it's floor-to-ceiling festering with mould. It stinks something fierce – stale and rotten, that species of stink you can taste, that you can actually taste at the back of your mouth. I'm frightened to breathe in. What if there are spores and stuff? What if there are germs or specks of fungus floating around? What if it gets in me?

Also, teensy detail, but all of downstairs is totally flooded.

And I mean ultra-flooded. The water reaches three-quarters of the way up the staircase. A couple of metres deeper and it'd pretty much splash against the ceiling of the downstairs hallway.

Plus the water keeps rising, keeps rising, it keeps on rising. It gushes from the open door of Mum's room, all the water from all the streams and torrents from the bazillion houses above. It sprays down the walls. It showers from cracks in the ceiling. The house is loud as a rainstorm, and the air is stifling. Steamy. Smothering.

The gloom doesn't help. All the lights are on, yet the mildew-coated bulbs shine a strange dull green – green mixed with blue. The mouldy walls glisten moistly in the weird dingy light.

Then I gasp and shrink back from the walls as that's when I spot that they're covered in eggs: not normal eggs, but Shade Girl's creepy, frogspawny ones. They're stuck in gloopy clusters to what remains of the wallpaper, tongues of slime dribbling beneath them, like they've been spat there. They squirm. They pulse in the blue-green light, and there are some on the ceiling too.

I'm trapped with them. It doesn't matter how fast I go and how far behind Shade Girl is because I'm stuck, and there's nowhere – absolutely nowhere – else to run. Nowhere else to even swim.

I collapse on the soaking, disgusting carpet.

'Oh God. Oh God.'

I'm out of breath. I'm suddenly so exhausted that I don't know if I can get back up.

Then something happens that floods me with both relief and dread, and I hug trembling arms round my sweat-painted chest.

It's Mum's bedroom. More exactly, it's the door to Mum's bedroom.

It closes. By itself.

Then, one blink later, there's no door there at all, but just another damp, festering wall – and what does it mean, what does it actually, literally mean? That something's looking out for me? Is my house looking out for me and trying to keep me safe?! Because, unless she can claw her way through the newly formed wall, Shade Girl can't get me any more. She can't get me. And it dawns on me that I can't feel the being-watched sensation either.

Then again, Shade Girl doesn't need to get me. There's nowhere else to go after all, plus the water still keeps rising, keeps rising, it keeps on rising. Shade Girl is NOT my only problem right now. Or maybe Shade Girl's the one who trapped me here on the landing in the first place . . .

I don't think so, though. I narrow my eyes at the newly formed wall and size it up: yet, no matter how much I look at it, the wall doesn't make my stomach squirm in the way that Shade Girl does. In its own fungusy way, I think my house really is watching out for me . . .

My vision swirls. I cough from the mildew-stench. Then I sit up straighter, clutch my chest, catch my breath, and my hair clings horribly to my forehead.

A shooting pain leaps up my left leg.

I wince and look down. Through the rip in one of my pyjama bottoms, I see that the scar has turned from white to deep, furious blue, and that the skin all around it has gone pale.

My mouth tastes throw-uppy; I shake all over and look away. But, try as I might, I can't ignore how the scar prickles and how badly it itches – LORD it itches – like Shade Girl ripped open the cut again and shoved singing sting-sting leaves from Voxminer against it. I grit my teeth. It stings sooo bad.

I still don't look at it, but breathe in as much as deeply utterly absolutely possible, and I don't care about spores in the rancid air any more.

I shut my eyes and focus not on my leg but the tug-on-my-heart.

There has to be a way out of this. Ben was sure of it. The tug-on-my-heart seemed certain about it.

'Please,' I whisper to the tug. 'Show me a way out. Pleeease.'

Then I feel it.

I feel the way home.

To my surprise, the tug-on-my-heart's not saying to head down any more.

Forward, it seems to say instead. You need to swim forward. Keep going, Lori.

My stomach churns with confusion. But the tug was right about the cupboard under the stairs – kind of? Sort of? So is it right about this as well?

What choice do I even have?

Swallowing, I peer down the mould-carpeted steps at the flooded downstairs hallway. The water sloshes. It's almost nearly reached the very top steps, and splashes echo wildly in the cramped, boiling space that is the upstairs landing. But now that I look again, actually for real look, I notice, with a soul-leaping thrill, that the downstairs hallway doesn't end with yet another weird wall where the front door should be. In fact, it doesn't seem to end at all. It just keeps going and going until it's totally swallowed by darkness – darkness so dark that, if this was Voxminer, it would be totally infested with gloom guzzlers.

That's where the tug-on-my-heart is leading me.

Into the shadows.

My bad leg twitches. Under my bare feet, mould and water mix on the carpet into a vile paste.

Tears stream down my cheeks. They mingle with steam and sweat and mist.

. . . How did any of this HAPPEN?

Why me? Why does Shade Girl want me? How did I get sucked into this weirdo nightmare? Why, why do I have to face it alone? Why did I have to be alone tonight? Why the flipping literal heck did I WANT to be alone?!

GOD, I wish I was being haunted by Fireplace Dave! Some regular, run-of-the-mill ghost that, yeah, sure, probably shouldn't exist, but which I could at least understand!

I wish none of this had happened. I wish I didn't have to deal with this. I wish it with every last bit of my absolute soul.

But then I curl my fingers round an imaginary hand.

Shoelace's hand.

Sobs catch in my throat.

'Shoelace,' I whisper. My voice cracks. My tears double. Triple. Quadruple. 'Shoelace.'

I wish Shoelace was with me. I wish she was here so, so bad . . .

But then I wipe my tears because at least I know she's waiting for me.

'M-move, Lori,' I breathe to myself. 'K-keep going.'

With all the effort in the literal galaxy, I push myself to my feet, then take my rucksack off, fish out my swimming costume and stare at it in my water-wrinkled fingers. It's a one-piece, bright blue, with three neon pink stripes on the left-hand side that run from top to bottom. It's plain-looking. It was absolutely NOT my first choice.

'But almost-teenagers,' Mum said when we were out shopping for it at the end of summer and a couple of lifetimes ago, 'don't wear Voxminer swimsuits. Wouldn't you agree, hmm?' And, suddenly,

I had to prove to her how grown-up I was. That meant choosing something with no cartoons on it. It meant nothing with Detective Mermaid, and none of the cats from Monster Kitten Fighting Force either.

Suddenly I can't help smiling a bit.

'Thanks, Mum,' I whisper, and I mean it. Because, though I still utterly wish I'd chosen something with Riley from Shimmer Squad on it, thank goodness, at least, Mum didn't let me get a Voxminer swimsuit. I think, for now, I'm juuust about done with video games . . . I could go a month or so without them . . . a week or two . . .

As fast as possible – and with the being-watched feeling no longer an issue – I take my pyjamas off, drop them on the floor, then pull on my swimming costume in the misty blue-green air.

CHAPTER 7

I didn't realise how wet my pyjamas were, how heavy they were, how they clung to every last single part of me like a second skin. I don't take them off so much as peel them off. But, once I'm in my swimming costume, I'm a thousand times lighter. And, though the air is rotten and sauna-moist, now that my arms and legs are bare and free, I'm calmer.

Usually, when I'm about to swim, I get a rush – a rush of complete total excitement that I'm about to dive in the water and take first place!

But maybe it isn't so weird that, this time, I'm calm instead of excited. Because my swimsuit makes me feel normal. Like the landing is just another changing room, that the water cascading from the ceiling is the noise of showers, and I'm about to take part in just-another-race.

I feel like myself. More myself than I've been in hours. And, with the warm air wrapping round my skin, I'm reminded again of how I love my miracle body.

My body is a miracle. I am a miracle. A complete and total MIRACLE.

My hands tremble.

I can't stop staring at my soaking blue pyjama top by my feet on the sodden carpet, at my torn pyjama bottoms, and at my Detective Mermaid rucksack that I don't reckon I'm ever going to see again. It helps distract from the lightning pain in my left leg.

The air feels even hotter, wetter, as sticky as marsh glue in Voxminer. My breath clouds. I tap a wet foot against the putrid floor, and it goes splat-splat-splat.

My hair sticks hideously to my back.

I shut my eyes for a second – then I make up my mind about something, open my eyes again, and reach for my rucksack. It's meant to be waterproof, yet the air's so heavy, so utterly ludicrously wet, that, inside, all my clothes are soaked right through, and my Shimmer Squad books have basically turned into papery mush.

I find my Monster Kitten pencil case and pull out the dolphin-themed safety scissors. And, before I can change my mind back, I drop the rucksack on the floor again, along with my pencil case, stand up straight as a stick-beast in Voxminer, and whisper, 'Here goes . . .'

Then I cut off all my hair past my shoulders.

It's hard; I wince the whole time; dolphin-themed safety scissors are NOT the perfect scissors for cutting hair with. But, suddenly, it's done, and I stare at wet clumps of my long brown hair just lying there, lying on the floor, and my hands are shaky and my breath turns giddy and I feel lighter than ever.

I put the scissors down and touch my new haircut. I feel how short it is . . .

I gulp.

Then I face the flood.

The surface is choppy. Waterfalls still pour down the mouldy walls and from the egg-glooped ceiling. But in the choppy water I catch little snatches of my own reflection.

'Your leg,' my reflection seems to say. 'Look at your leg. Look at it. Look at it.'

I shake my head and try not to gaze at the blue horror on my left leg. Instead, I concentrate on the tug, that mysterious tug-on-my-heart that urges me down the steps.

'G-get back home,' I tell myself. 'Mum'll take you to hospital. They'll sort out your leg. You have to get back first, though.'

Very, very, very slowly, I dip my right big toe in the water. It's warm as a Friday-night bath.

. . . Does this count as a bath? Does this mean I'm finally following ground rule number two from a million years ago?

I'm not sure. With all the flecks of mould that float in the water, it's not exactly clean. More to the point, if I'm not in the tub, and if I've still got clothes on, I don't reckon it counts.

But! Do swimming costumes count as clothes? Like . . . they're not-not clothes, but also something about calling them clothes feels wrong?

Maybe I'll talk about it with Shoelace.

I grin.

Oh my goodness. I can't WAIT to be with Shoelace again and talk about dumb, random thoughts that don't even matter and which aren't even important!

I dunk my whole right leg into the water, then my left leg, too, which stings, though the pain dulls almost at once. Then I enter the flood fully and keep my feet on the steps for as long as humanly aquatically possible.

Soon the water is neck-deep. Two steps after that, I'm right on the tips of my toes.

Then I'm floating in the bath-warm lake that floods all of downstairs, and my stomach swoops. Water presses round my body in a tight hug. It's normally my favourite feeling in the world – a swimming-pool sensation, like the water knows me, supports me, envelops me.

This water, though, feels different. It doesn't smell of chlorine. It doesn't smell much of anything, or maybe I just can't catch its scent over the gagging stench from the walls and ceiling.

But though the water feels different from normal, though it's dotted with mould, I sense that it's still my friend. That it's worried for me. Terrified for me.

'Lori,' I imagine the water whispering. 'You're not safe in me. Swim fast. Swim silent.'

I scowl. The water keeps rising, keeps rising, it keeps on rising. My short, scruffy hair nearly brushes the mucusy ceiling.

'Keep going!' the water seems to say.

The further I swim, the darker the downstairs hallway gets, and it's hard to keep quiet. My splashes are sooo loud in the tiny space.

'Keep going!'

If I reached upwards, I could touch the eggs that cling to the ceiling. Not that I want to, of course. Because yuck.

'Keep going!'

How long does the hallway last? What if it floods completely before I reach the exit? What if I get trapped? What if I've already gone way too far to get back to the landing in time?

'Keep going,' I say to myself.

Mould-speckled water gets in my mouth, and I gag, but I don't care. I don't care. I need to hear my own voice.

'Keep going!'

The end comes

suddenly.

One instant, I'm in the hallway, swimming into darkness built for gloom guzzlers. The next, the cramped hallway is gone, and I'm in open water surrounded by fog. I don't even smack into the front door. There is no front door.

I gasp, turn round, look back behind me. The sudden fog is so wildly thick, though, that it's already swallowed the hallway. I can't see it any more. And the air's no longer rainstorm-loud, but snoozefinder-quiet. For all I know, I could be infinity miles from anywhere.

Yet a flash of warmth lights in my heart, and the warmth travels through my blood and all the way under my skin. In my head, a huge enormous thought blazes in thousand-metre writing. Three words. Just three short words, yet they are the BIGGEST words.

I DID IT.

I actually, for real, not-even-joking DID IT.

I beam and I beam and I BEAM.

'I got out,' I splutter. 'Jonesy. Ben. Mum. Shoelace. I did it. I got out.'

At least, I'm 99 per cent sure I did. I'm 99 per cent sure this isn't some cruel, weird trick.

I glance around at the mysterious fog, and my smile flickers only a bit.

Wherever I've ended up, it's an improvement at least.

Even if leaving the house means I've finally broken all ten of Mum's ground rules.

CHAPTER 6

My smile sinks, and my heart beats fast again. Even if this is an improvement, I'm not sure, suddenly, how much good it does me.

For starters, where in the world have I escaped to?

I bob in the water and look around again. The water is warm, and there's not even a single speck of mildew in it any more. The mouldy stench of the rotten-foul air has gone – so, for the first time, I realise the water does have its own smell, and that its smell is stitched from all things soft and sweet-tastic. The water even tastes sweet, like cherries, and the tug-on-my-heart urges me to keep swimming forward through the cherry-cheered water.

Where 'forward' actually leads, I've got nooo idea. The fog still surrounds me. It surrounds me COMPLETELY, and it's sickly-looking. I don't like how it glows the same dull blue-green as the lights in the flooded version of my house.

But I guess I'm thankful for the dimly shining fog since it also hides me. It hides me from her.

I can feel her gaze again.

I feel *Shade Girl*.

For a second, I go ultra-extremely still and just drift in the warm, sweet water. And, from somewhere beyond the fog, I feel the being-watched sensation.

There's something off about it. It's desperate. Frantic. It keeps passing over me, like it only has a rough idea where I am.

I frown. How on actual earth could I possibly know that Shade Girl's far-off gaze keeps passing over me? That doesn't make sense. It makes no sense at all. That's not something you can feel! Yet, with every swoosh in my belly and thrill in my blood, I get more and more certain that, as long as I stay quiet and the fog keeps hiding me, maybe I've got the teeniest little chance of getting home.

'Mum. Shoelace,' I whisper. 'I'm coming.'

My left leg is on fire. Every single part of me kills. But I force myself to swim again.

I'm slow, frustratingly slow – I usually swim waaay faster than this. But I don't dare push myself harder because I can't see more than perhaps half a metre through the fog, and I've got no idea what's out there. I don't know how far it is until land – I have to save my energy. I can't tell how deep the water is either. Maybe it's the same as the deep end of me and Shoelace's local swimming pool, or perhaps it plunges for miles and miles into monster-ruled blackness, into some kingdom of teeth and tentacles.

I picture crush-cruncher from Voxminer, with its big squishy head and all those suckers. I imagine swarms of eel-blades slicing through the blackness, then I think of leviatitan (le-VIA-titan), which has six vast mouths and a hundred tentacles and a bazillion million teeth, and is the biggest Voxfriend of all entire time.

My breath shudders; I keep my gaze straight ahead as best I can. I don't want to think about beasts in the deep. I don't want to think about sleeping terrors with mouths big enough to swallow a girl whole.

Quickly, so quickly that I don't see it coming,
I reach the edge of the fog bank
and emerge under a gazillion stars.

My eyes go wide, and my arms go limp. In front of me, the sea stretches forever like a black, black mirror, like the place in Voxminer with all the eggs in it. The sky is nothing like I've ever seen. I am the tiniest tiny thing that has absolutely ever existed in human history.

Oh wow . . . I mouth.

Deep down, I know I should be scared. I think of the freakish eggs hatching in Voxminer, of a hundred million copies of myself chasing after Ben and RoaryCat11.

Yet, in that moment, I'm not scared. I'm not even worried that I'm in the open, where Shade Girl's gaze might land on me at any second. I'm too small to be worried. I'm so small that I suddenly reckon nothing could spot me in a thousand years of searching.

It's night-time, but the sky isn't black, not entirely. The spots that are black are the deepest, purest, most absolute dark you could ever dream of in your life. But, between the dark patches, huge swathes of the titanic sky are painted with splashes of shining mist, and the mists are a hundred different colours: mauve and scarlet, navy, rich pink like cupcake crystals in Voxminer and forest-biome green. It's a patchwork night, and the patchwork is sewn from magic.

And all across the patchwork sky are a gazillion million stars, and the stars gleam every last single colour I could ever even think of. They are red and they are yellow and they are blue and green and pink and orange and purple and white. They are Christmas-light stars. Treasure-chest stars that glisten bright as jewels in the hoard of a smoulder dragon, aka the greediest Voxfriend in Voxminer.

I'm smaller, smaller, smaller than ever. I can't rip my gaze from the stars. I can't take my eyes from the shimmering mists of the night.

I've seen photos of mists like this in science books. They're called nebula (or is that nebulas? Nebuli? Glimmerings of nebula?). They're like giant nests where young stars are born, and you find them in deepest outer space. Normally, you'd need a big old telescope to see them, yet here they take up half the sky.

The more I stare, the more I feel I'm being drawn up, up, up into the impossibly starry night.

The stars reach down for me. They scoop me from the water and form a path for me, a glittering trail into the sky—

and the air smells sweet

it tastes of sugar

I giggle

I run

the stars dance

they sing my name

Lori Lori Lori

they twist into galaxies

they want to turn my skin into stars

my bones into light
and for the stars of my body
to join the Dance,
the Dance that began
at the Beginning of Time.
I shriek with laughter!
I put on speed
I race up the path
into the night,
I'm surrounded
by joy
and light
and colour
and colour
and colour
and colour—

the path winds
I hurry faster
I'm a golden comet
a flash of light
I'm dashing
along crystal trails
of winding starshine,
and at the end
of the jewel path
I spy the whitest light,
the brightest light yet,

blinding

brilliant

LIGHT

CHAPTER 5

Pain detonates in my scar, plunges me right back down to the water.

I scream! Wince! Sob! But then I swallow the pain down as best I can and paddle hard, suddenly scared once more of leviatitans in the deep.

'Keep going!' urges the tug-on-my-heart. 'Don't look at the stars – don't fall for their song, don't be lured by the Dance. Don't listen to them. Don't fall behind.'

At once, I peer at the stars again. They twinkle innocently in the patchwork night.

Did I . . . did I just dream all of that? Did any of that with the stars really happen?!

My head goes light, in that nasty way when you feel a cold coming on. Despite how real all of it seemed, I don't think it actually happened. I think it was like my nightmare from earlier. It just felt like it happened, when, in reality, I'm 95 per cent sure I was simply drifting in the water the whole time, half asleep from how exhausted I am. I was imagining things. Hallucinating or something.

I think.

I *think*.

I want to cry, but I have to keep going. So I give the stars one last suspicious little glare, then keep my head down, fight the pain that now shoots up the whole left side of my body and start swimming again.

'Keep going,' says the tug-on-my-heart. 'Keep going. Keep going.'

I swim deeper into the black-mirror ocean. It's like helioserpents are wriggling in my ribcage, and there are eel-blades in my stomach. Everything feels weird. Everything hurts.

And I try not to think how the scar on my leg must look by now, how much bluer it's probably got since I entered the water back on the mould-festering landing. Instead, I think about how Shade Girl already showed me this place in Voxminer, or something close to it.

I swim faster.

It KILLS to swim faster. The stinging's spread to everywhere below my stomach. It covers my belly and both my legs and my feet and also my toes. My mouth is full of the cherry sweetness of the water. My nostrils dance with a scent like sugar.

I love sweets, but oceans shouldn't smell like this.

Shoelace, I mouth. Think of Shoelace.

I grit my teeth. Keep on swimming.

Mum and Shoelace are my light.

In fact, in the distance, I suddenly SEE a light shining super bright just above the water. Is it a star? A planet?

Whatever it is, it's small and golden, plus it wasn't there before. I know at once that it's where the tug-on-my-heart is leading.

Mum. Shoelace.

The stinging crawls above my stomach. It jabs at my arms.

Mum. Shoelace.

I don't want to die. I don't want to die.

Mum. Shoelace.

The stars are bright. The water reflects them so perfectly that it's like there are two night skies: one above and one below. I swim through starlight.

Mum.

I'm surrounded by glimmerings of nebula. By sweetness. By endless colour.

Shoelace.

The colours

twist and swirl,

the water surrounds my body,

and I hear voices, voices in my mind.

'Keep going,' I imagine Mum saying to me.

'You're sooo close, Roars!' an imaginary Shoelace puts in.

'Keep going!

'Keep going!

'KEEP GOING!'

I gasp hugely, and it's the breath of my whole entire life! And, suddenly, I've closed the distance. The bright light is right ahead of me. I can see what it is.

It's a doorway.

An exit.

CHAPTER 4

There are stairs, too.

They rise from the sea, and they're made from something like blue-grey marble, or like how fissure-stone looks when you find it deep underground in magma chambers in Voxminer. I count seven, eight, nine tall steps, all of them wide enough for a grown-up to comfortably climb, and all with murderously sharp edges. On the very top step, the open doorway waits for me, and the inside of the frame blazes with golden light.

The water is warmer than ever, and it smells sweeter than ever, too. It's calm. Freakishly calm. The door and the stairs are reflected absolutely perfectly in the mirror of the ocean.

I stop swimming just before the first step. Tense up. Listen to the tug-on-my-heart, which utterly swears to me that, no matter how soul-clenching this place feels, this isn't a trap.

'Up!' the tug says. 'Hurry, Lori. Up! Hurry!'

I drag my arms from the water. Haul myself on to the stairs.

Exhaustion SLAMS into me, beats me down, makes me gasp! My vision blackens round the edges. I close my eyes tightly, but that's almost worse since it makes me focus on the vomity taste that slops up my throat.

I open my eyes again.

My body has changed.

I don't mean to look at my scar – I don't want to even THINK about my scar – but I glance at it by accident, and now I HAVE to look because my scar shines navy. It must also have infected the rest of me because my skin's gone see-through, not just on my leg but all over me and under my swimming costume, too, I think. Yet the thing that makes me feel most awful wretched nasty putrid rancid is that, though I can see under my skin, I can't see my bones. I don't seem to have any muscles or guts. It's like I've been remade from the stuff of a jellyfish.

But, though I don't have bones or muscles or guts, I still have a heart, and my heart shines navy, too. I see it. I see it pound and pound under my swimming costume. Blooming from my luminous blue heart and criss-crossing over my skin are what look like veins – yet it's not blood that pulses through them but liquid starlight or something. Whatever the stuff is, it glows faintly silver – silvery-blue. If it wasn't so wrong-looking, it would be as pretty as heart-star.

Trembling, I lift up a jelly-like finger. I press it slowly against the milky see-throughness of my arm.

'OUCH!'

My skin is soft and cold and wet, like how I imagine slithering creatures in the sliming, shuddering deep must feel. It hurts. It's like I don't touch myself with a squishy fingertip, but fully stab myself with a kitchen knife.

I whip my finger away, but the pain doesn't fade. My breath rasps, even though I don't have lungs; my throat gurgles, even though I'm not 100 per cent sure I still have a throat. And I stare in horror at where I touched myself: the skin has turned a vivid, bitter purple.

It's too much. I can't deal with this. I can't, I can't, I can't, I can't.

I curl up on the bottom step.

Yet, even now, the tug-on-my-navy-shining-heart urges me up the stairs.

'Lori!' I feel it saying. 'You're so close! Keep going!'

The tug gives me juuust enough energy to drag my sopping body wetly up the stairs. The steps are warm. They're so insanely smooth that they're hard to hold on to. But my body is sticky, so I manage it, and after a million years I finally reach the top.

I stop again to catch my breath.

I think of Shade Girl dragging herself across the carpet. I grit my teeth, but my teeth feel squelchy. Jelly-like.

Mum. Shoelace.

The open door rises above me. I don't know where it goes, but the light feels warm. My heart says it leads to either Mum or Shoelace.

Mum. Shoelace.

In my mouth, the vomity taste turns sweet.

Mum. Shoelace.

My brain is as soft as swamp gunk from Voxminer. Maybe I am swamp gunk. Maybe that's what I'm turning into, and I don't even have a brain any more, or a skull, or hair, or any of the stuff that makes me me.

. . . The warmth is nice. It's nice, here, at the top of the stairs . . .

Mum. Shoelace.

Maybe I should curl up a while longer. Get my strength back.

Mum.

The air is sweet, and my body is jelly and wriggles and pulses, and I feel it pulsing. Warm, sweet life pumps through my starlight veins. I love it. I love how it feels.

Shoelace.

My swamp-gunk body is full of life and sweetness.

Shoelace.

I shut my eyes and imagine Shade Girl's eggs hatching, and for the hatchlings to find me warm and waiting at the top of the stairs for them. The brood won't have trouble finding me. I know they won't – because, suddenly, and with heart-star gleaming certainty, I understand I belong to them. I'm theirs, their first-ever meal in the world. I exist to make them strong.

My body will make for fine feeding indeed.

Something twists in my heart.

I want to be their first-ever meal. I want to make for good feeding. With all my soul, with all my very utter soul, I WANT this.

I imagine a thousand scurrying creatures with long arms and spindly little legs, drawn to me through the warm, sweet air.

My heart smiles.

Shoelace.

My body is sticky as marsh glue. My jelly-wet skin clings to the blue-grey surface.

A beautiful thought comes to me. I sob from golden happiness.

I can stick myself to the steps! If I push down as much as I can, I'll stick so hard to them that nothing could prise me away, nothing, nothing at all! Nothing can keep me from being the brood's first meal!

. . . Shoelace . . .

I am a feast-in-waiting: I exist for Shade Girl's hatchlings. They are the only things that matter in the whole universe.

What, on the entire planet of Planet Earth, is 'Shoelace'?

I hear the squelch of my heart in my jelly-sticky body.

Shoelace.

Is Shoelace a name or something? Whatever it is, it's also a splinter. It's sharp. I hate it. I hate how the word stabs at me. Yet something in my heart says that to get rid of Shoelace – to make things right again – I have to ooze just a tiiiny bit closer to the light, the golden light that's the only thing I can still see with my eyes sealed shut.

Shoelace.

My breath is a spluttering gurgle. I don't want to do this. I don't want to move. But, if moving towards the light will get rid of Shoelace, I'll do it for the brood.

I push myself closer.

Shoelace.

The golden light is warm, bright. I slosh a little closer . . .

Closer . . .

Closer . . .

I tumble into a bedroom and GASP.

Artwork to come

Where I leap through

a door for you

CHAPTER 3

I'm myself again so suddenly that my brain splits in two. I SCREAM.

Something like lightning shoots through my body, from the plates of my skull to the ribs of my chest, the discs of my spine, the bones of my arms and fingers and legs.

Then, at once, my skin is pale pink and freckly, and it's warm and it's solid, and I can feel my bones in me, and I can feel my muscles, and nothing stings any more, and I'm on all fours on a soft red carpet. I'm retching. I'm dripping wet. My swimming costume clings miserably to my body, and my heart hammers so fast that it hurts.

I don't care, though. I don't even care how awful I feel.

I love it. My breath catches, and there are tears in my eyes, and they're fat and wet, and they splash on the floor. I love it. I LOVE it.

The pain means I'm ME again!!

. . . Soft red carpet . . .

I know this carpet. I know these colouring pencils thrown

about, and I know these scruffy sketchbooks and Big City Kitty manga comics scattered everywhere. I know this plastic toy Voxminer sword with rainbow shoelaces tied round the hilt.

I smile at the sword. 'Could've done with you tonight,' I whisper.

Then I sit up and wipe my eyes and look round Shoelace's bedroom.

Her room is waaay bigger than mine, and the ceiling is higher and covered in glow-in-the-dark stars, but not like the ones they sell at Save Shoppers, but awesome realistic ones that look like the actual night sky (not that I can see them very well with the lamp on). The walls are newly painted in pastel pink. The floor is messy, and not just with art stuff but with toys and drawings of Kittentopia, and cool anime pictures of our player characters in Voxminer. Shoelace's heavy, plush curtains are shut. A streetlamp shines orangely through the gap in the curtains. It's still the middle of the night.

A silver waste-paper bin glints near Shoelace's fancy new desk.

Before I know it, I'm crouching over the bin and throwing up among pencil shavings and balls of scrunched-up paper. My nose wrinkles. I don't look in the bin because the stuff I've vomited is like black sludge, and it reeks like sewage.

But, despite the deathly stink, my heart calms, and my stomach turns nearly normal-feeling again, and I collapse on Shoelace's carpet. I stare up at her big light, then at the large sticker-coated wardrobe from which I stumbled.

The wardrobe is open. Through it, I see the black-mirror ocean. I see endless stars glitter-twinkling.

I hear voices.

Snatches of voices.

They sound raised, yet also super muffled: they're from way downstairs. But I listen as hard as I can, and, muffled or not, I recognise the voices of Shoelace's parents.

'Oh, for heaven's sake, Charlie. Did you leave LumiTube on again?'

'Hey! I haven't even watched any LumiTube tonight!'

(It's Shoelace. Shoelace is shouting, oh God, oh my actual God. Shoelace is right downstairs, right this literal instant!)

'Don't argue with your father, Charlie. Go upstairs and turn it off.'

'It IS off!'

Her parents blatantly don't believe her, though. So, a second later, I hear someone thump up two flights of stairs, and it sounds awfully like how Shoelace always thumps up the stairs . . .

I scramble to my feet.

The door swings open.

There stands Shoelace.

There she is, there she actually for real is, scowling in scarlet Voxminer pyjamas in the light of the second-floor landing. Her usually straight hair is messy, and her eyes are red. She's obviously been crying a whole ton.

But now her eyes go totally wide, and she gawps at me.

I don't know whether to laugh or cry. Instead, I give her a sheepish little wave, then whisper, 'Um . . . mind if I sleep over tonight?'

Shoelace doesn't answer. She doesn't even answer. She just swallows, and her eyes turn redder, and she's crying again – she's properly sobbing. And even though I must be a sight – randomly in my dripping swimsuit in her fancy new bedroom and next to the sludge-bin – she strides up and hugs me, holds me so tight that she squeezes the breath from me, and she doesn't care that I'm soaking wet because then she hugs me even more. I don't reckon she's going to let me go ever, ever, ever.

I don't want her to.

'Sh-Shoelace!' I gasp, but she cuts me off.

'Shut it. Just hug me back, yeah?'

I hurl my arms round her, and she's solid and she's real and she's there. She's there – my Shoelace! My Shoelace, who smells of the marshmallow bubble bath she always makes her parents buy!

It is the best and greatest smell in the total universe.

'R-Roars,' Shoelace half sobs, half whispers in my ear, 'I . . . I tried showing them. I tried showing everyone. But my laptop, it – it switched itself off. It won't turn on again. Then Voxminer wouldn't open on my Game Galaxy either for some reason, and – and–' Her voice breaks. 'No one believed what I said.'

'No kidding,' I whisper back. Then I do my impression of her that always drives her nuts. "'Mum! Dad! Lori's trapped in another world! Let's go save her, yeah?'"

Shoelace giggle-sobs. I know her well enough to guess that, though that's probably not exactly what she said to her parents, it's prooobably not far off either.

She lets go of me. Stares at me in wonder.

Then she nods at me and says, 'Nice hair. Ben cut it?'

I laugh and feel my short, safety-scissors-cut hair. I don't even answer her. I'm just . . . happy. I'm happy.

Shoelace grabs my hand. 'C'mon,' she says. 'We need to tell Mum and Dad.'

But instead of dragging me downstairs she shuffles on the spot, and I know she's thinking the same as me.

'Let's . . . give it another second,' I say.

I squeeze her hand – and she smiles and nods back. Because this, right now, this is a moment just for us and no one else.

At last, Shoelace spots the ocean in her wardrobe. She lets go of me, takes a slow step towards it, and a shining smile takes over her face.

'That's – that's—'

'The suckiest place ever,' I tell her. 'Trust me. My review is, like, minus a million out of ten.'

Shoelace shakes her head. 'But Roars, that's – that's another world.'

I roll my eyes. 'Yep. Sure is.'

'No, Roars, seriously. Another world. In my wardrobe, Roars!'

She claps her hands a little. I want to roll my eyes again, but somehow I find myself grinning. Now she's over the shock of discovering me in her room, I should've known this is how she'd react.

My grin doesn't last, though, since a tropical breeze blows from the open wardrobe. It scatters the drawings of Kittentopia littering the floor. It's scorching, yet it makes me shiver.

We're wasting time. Shade Girl could appear at any second.

But I can't bring myself to take even a single step towards the wardrobe.

'Can you just shut it already?' I whisper.

Shoelace nods firmly. But she also fumbles in one of her pyjama pockets, pulls out her phone and says, 'Hang on, hang on. Just need a picture.'

'Shoelace, you've really got to—'

'One sec!'

'Shoelace—'

'Argh, phone's almost out of battery. Won't let me take it.'

The sweltering breeze boils. My chest burns powerfully cold with fear.

I snatch her phone away and toss it on her bed. 'Shoelace!' I snap.

Our eyes meet. Shoelace gulps and purses her lips. This close, I see her cheeks redden, or at least as much as they can with how dark her skin is.

'Um . . . guess I don't need a photo,' she says, a teeny bit sheepishly. 'Should we, er, shut it together?'

A wave of heat rises in my own cheeks.

'S-sorry. God, Shoelace, I – I didn't mean to snap. Really. I just—'

There's a pause. I want to tell her I'm sorry again, that I'm so – that I'm just so . . . nervous. On edge. All I want is for tonight to be done.

But Shoelace smiles and squeezes my hand and, with nothing but her eyes, she says, Don't even worry about it, yeah? And it makes me want to hug her all over again.

I swallow and nod. 'Okay,' I whisper. 'Let's do it together . . .'

Then, as one, we face the wardrobe.

Except, suddenly, the world beyond the wardrobe changes.

Through the door, the stars turn red, the glimmerings of nebula go scarlet, and the ocean goes from black to deep, deep red.

It's not that, however, that makes me gasp, but the bone-white fingers that reach through the open wardrobe.

Spider's fingers.

There's a low-throated growl.

A long, terrible arm, thin but strong, and fast.

Shoelace shrieks as Shade Girl wraps crushing fingers round her waist. The fingers are so long that they reach all the way round her belly.

Shoelace's parents yell from downstairs.

'CHARLIE! WHAT'S WRONG?'

Shoelace doesn't even get a chance to scream back. Shade Girl just yanks her through the wardrobe like a doll.

My ears ring.

I heave.

I stare.

I hear Shoelace's parents run up the stairs. And, from nowhere, I have the choice of my absolute entire life to make.

All night long, I have battled to get home. I have faced monsters. Darkness. I almost died tonight. So, with every inch of my heart, every millimetre of my soul, I can't face Shade Girl again. I completely utterly CAN'T.

But that doesn't matter the slightest little bit, because I can't live without Shoelace.

Without waiting for Shoelace's parents,

I make my choice and

throw myself

through

the

open

wardrobe.

CHAPTER 2

Before, the ocean smelled sweet, but now it does not. The instant I'm through the wardrobe, I'm walloped by a gasping stench like rancid fruit, a reek that would make Shoelace's sludge-ridden waste-paper bin smell as good as her bubble bath in comparison. I clap a hand over my mouth to stop from retching.

And the heat.

The air is so heavy that it crushes my lungs. It's so stuffy that I can barely take it. I'm already sweating buckets.

But I have to take it. If I don't, I'll lose my best-friend-forever, forever.

'SHOELACE!'

It's hard to see, hard to make things out in the dull red light of the stars above – but Shoelace is at the bottom of the staircase, on the final step just above the ocean. She's on her back. She's shaking. I can't see Shade Girl anywhere, but I spy ripples in the blood-red ocean, like something revulsive just slid beneath the surface.

Shoelace pushes herself back up, then rushes up the wide, steep steps. I hurry down to her. We meet halfway up the staircase, and her eyes sparkle with tears.

'Wh-where's Shade Girl?' I splutter.

Shoelace points at the ripples. 'It let go of me!' she gasps. She wipes her forehead. She's sweating, too. 'I dunno why.'

I swallow, but help Shoelace up the steps as fast as I can, back to the door.

Except I suddenly realise why Shade Girl let go of her. I realise why Shade Girl can take her time with us.

The door no longer leads anywhere.

The frame remains: a large grey-blue rectangle on the ninth step, aka the very top of the staircase – yet it's now completely, totally empty. You can see stars through it. They glitter in the scarlet night.

I clutch Shoelace's hand. Peer into her terrified eyes.

'Oh God. Shoelace. I'm sorry.'

The words slip from me, but Shoelace won't hear them. 'Not your fault, dummy,' she says.

I shake my head. 'I should've shut your wardrobe. I should've shut it before you even reached your bedroom. I – I should've—'

Shoelace grabs my shoulders and shakes me. 'ROARS!' she cries, and I'm amazed to see her smile. 'This! Isn't! Your! Fault!'

She says it so forcefully that I almost nearly believe her. Then she loosens her grip, and the worst thought in the history of everything crashes into my head.

'Shade Girl didn't cut you, did she?!'

Please say no. Anything but that. Pleeease.

Shoelace shakes her head. Golden relief shines in my heart. It only lasts for one split instant, though, for the air grows hotter than ever, and my mind turns clammy from the sticky heat.

Around us, the ocean churns.

It's not much, not to begin with: a handful of splashes on both sides of the staircase. But then me and Shoelace huddle close as we can because, seconds later, the splashes get bigger, and it's like the whole ocean boils. It bubbles like water in a saucepan.

Fear explodes through my skin as I understand what we're seeing.

These aren't bubbles. They're eggs: eggs rising from the blood-drenched deep to the scarlet surface. Jelly-like eggs exactly like the ones that cling to Shade Girl's body, except that there are thousands of them, a hundred million bazillion of them.

If I hadn't made it to Shoelace's bedroom, would the eggs have hatched and fed on me? Would I have been an easy meal for hatchlings to eat, all squashy and jellyish, in the same way that babyfood is always mushy?

Is that what happened to Hazel all those years ago? Did Hazel try and escape? Did she make it to the stairs? Are me and Shoelace standing right where Hazel was eaten?!

My guts coil. Perhaps she did make it, perhaps she did manage to escape from Shade Girl, and Shade Girl was lying when she said that Hazel was hers for the taking. At least, I hope so. I one trillion per cent hope so. Because I can't bear thinking about the alternative.

I grasp Shoelace, and Shoelace grasps me back.

At last, Shade Girl reveals herself.

In the dim red light, we watch the razor tips of her spidery fingers emerge from the water. They grope at the bottom steps. They go tap-scratch-tap against the possibly-marble, possibly-fissure-stone-from-Voxminer.

Next she hauls her colossal egg-sac body on to the stairs, and her body sloshes and squelches and glistens with wetness. Her eggs splat against the steps. A couple peel off and plop into the water, and I hear the popping again, the pop-pop-pop of smaller eggs being crushed inside her.

Shade Girl's wheezing assaults my ears. Her stench is so bad that my vision blackens. The stink pummels me. I taste it on my tongue.

Me and Shoelace back up against the empty doorframe, but there's nowhere to go. The ocean is egg-swamped. Shade Girl is already halfway up the stairs, and she is gigantic.

Then me and Shoelace catch each other's gaze, and I know at once that Shoelace is thinking the same as me.

This is it. The end.

We're going to die.

CHAPTER

1

I don't want to die.

It's such a simple thought, yet it's the most hugely enormous thought in all entire existence. I feel it with every cell of my miracle body. I am eleven years old, and I don't want to die.

My breath shakes. My literal spirit shakes.

I don't say any of this to Shoelace, though, because all that's left to say is the one thing that still matters, the one bit of good I can still cling to. Something I've never said out loud before.

I swallow, then open my mouth.

'I love you,' I tell her. I say it right into her ear in a choking whisper. 'You're my best friend. I love you.'

And it's the truth. It is the very utter truth of my whole entire soul.

Shoelace holds me so close that I feel her heart against my chest, and it's like our heartbeats join into one.

She whispers back with a shake in her voice.

'Love you, too, Roars,' she says.

I smile, and sob, and it's a whole-body sob that raises gooseflesh down my back and over my belly and my arms and legs. I dig my fingernails into Shoelace so that I'm holding her as much as I can, I love her, I love her, I am never letting go of her. No force in the universe can make me let go of Shoelace.

Shade Girl growls and hauls herself up the stairs. I hear the sickening slop-plop-splosh of her putrid body.

I hold Shoelace closer, closer. 'I love you, I love you, I love you!' I tell her.

Then I scrunch my eyelids and wait for Shade Girl to slice us up, rip us apart, transform us into swamp gunk.

I wait.

Wait.

I wait some more . . .

A million centuries pass. A tiny thought tiptoes into my mind, nervous and uncertain of itself.

But the thought asks: What on total earth is taking so long?

Not letting go of Shoelace, I open my eyelids by the smallest amount possible – and Shade Girl isn't where I expect her to be, aka right on top of us with her arms raised, ready to butcher us into hatchling-ready slices. Instead, she's squelched her way back to the bottom step, the step just above the water, where she waits in a pulsing, shapeless heap.

Then I gasp and open my eyes fully as I realise that 'wait' is entirely the wrong word – because, even in the dim red light, I see her tremble. I see the jelly-like shells of her eggs wiggle, waggle and writhe.

Shade Girl is not simply waiting for us at the bottom of the stairs.

Shade Girl is cowering at the bottom of the stairs.

Confused, I let go of Shoelace. Why is Shade Girl cowering? Why does she look like she's in pain?

'Wh-what's it doing?!' Shoelace asks.

I don't answer, but take a step down towards Shade Girl.

Shade Girl flinches! Roars! She backs away again and splashes halfway into the water! And, around us, in the red-coloured ocean, the thousands of extra eggs quiver horrendously.

My heart hammer-pounds. I don't know how it happened, or why, or what in the universe it could possibly mean. But I know that it's the truth.

For some reason, Shade Girl is scared of me and Shoelace.

She's downright petrified of us.

I feel for Shoelace's hand behind me, and she grabs my fingers; Shade Girl flinches again, and just like that my thoughts slot into place. I make a guess, too, that when she reached through the wardrobe into Shoelace's bedroom she only meant to grab me – or, if not me in particular, then just one of us, and only one of us. A last-ditch attempt to snatch a fresh meal for her hatchlings before we closed the door between worlds . . .

In that moment, I know what I have to do. What me and Shoelace have to do.

'Shoelace,' I whisper, though I keep my gaze locked on Shade Girl. 'Remember in Voxminer when we found that nest of cactus-kitten eggs?'

I don't need to look at Shoelace to know she's staring at me like I've gone actually totally literally nuts.

'Um, Roars?'

'The mother came along!' I say breathlessly. 'She was level sixty! I thought I was a goner, but then you beat her and saved me!'

Of course she remembers saving me from the giant cactus-kitten. She never shuts up about it. She even got the whole thing on video and posted it in the Voxminer forums and got over forty comments on it!

I know Shoelace. I know what makes her smile. So, when I risk a glance back over my shoulder at her, I'm not surprised to see the corners of her mouth twitch upwards.

'It was wicked awesome, right?' she says. 'What's this got to do with anything?'

It's Shade Girl who answers.

Shoelace jumps as Shade Girl howls, and then I know for certain that my hunch is correct. Shoelace's mouth becomes an O as she figures it out, too.

The reason Shade Girl didn't mean for us both to be here is because she's a creature of absolute loneliness. Love is deadly to her.

'Love is power,' Ben had said, then he even showed me that love is power when he entered Jonesy and saved me back in the living room.

I remember, too, what Shade Girl herself said in my nightmare through the voice of Ms Newt. 'I could never stand love,' she'd said. 'I could never stand its light.'

Me and Shoelace love one another. I love her. I love her.

And that gives us power.

Shoelace comes down a step so that we stand side by side. We still clasp each other's hands. 'Remember the hair-dye incident in school?' she says slyly.

I giggle. Who doesn't remember when Mr Willow came in one day with pink hair? Me and Shoelace still laugh about it!

My heart races.

We take another step down the stairs. Shade Girl backs up again, almost fully into the water.

'Remember our first sleepover?' I say. 'With The Record?'

Shoelace quivers with excitement. 'Oh, Roars! I meant to say – I found the little diary we kept!'

My soul swoops. The diary! The minute-by-minute diary we made during the very first Record attempt!

'Where was it?!' I blurt.

'Under my bed,' Shoelace answers. Her grin could light up a whole school hall in a Fireplace-Dave-related blackout. 'In one of my old sketchbooks. Dunno how it got there.'

Shade Girl howls again, howls, howls, HOWLS. It's a sound out of nightmares, a screech from Hell—

Me and Shoelace keep advancing, and I love her, love her. We remember all the things we've ever done together, everything that makes us best friends, best friends in the universe, and how much fun we always have.

'Remember the potato clock?' I ask.

(Down the steps. Down the steps.)

Shoelace scoffs. 'The potato clock? Pfft. Pur-lease. I can go one better. Remember at the bowling alley with the floor-pizza?'

'Egh, gross!' I say. Thinking about the floor-pizza makes me queasy, so I try and steer things in another direction. 'Remember when we met? My first day in Year Three?'

(Down the steps! Down the steps!)

Shoelace drops her voice. Gets more serious. 'Can you imagine if Mr Grace hadn't sat you next to me?'

I hold her hand tighter, tight in a Shoelace kind of way. With Shoelace-firmness, I say, 'Wouldn't have mattered. We still would've been friends.'

Then I smile at her. Even if we die, at least we'll die together.

Shoelace beams back at me, and my stomach goes cold, yet it's a nice sort of cold like I've never felt, which makes me want to hold her hand even harder, harder, harder.

Shade Girl SCREAMS. She's so loud and so actually-really-human-sounding that me and Shoelace's courage finally snaps. We race back up the steps to the empty doorframe.

'ROARS!' Shoelace cries.

'SHOELACE!' I cry back.

But Shade Girl doesn't follow us. She gurgles in the water. She twists about, she squirms, she splashes – and the rancid orbs in the hearts of her eggs start to glow. They shine brighter and brighter, bright as stars.

The same thing happens with the eggs in the sea. They turn blinding. I shield my eyes and squint through my fingers; it's like the ocean is suddenly made from pure white light, or from heart-star, or from a trillion moonglow-lanterns!

Shade Girl shrieks again, and her scream pierces my soul. I keel over from the pain of it. So does Shoelace—

The screaming stops.

The lights go out across the whole sea – the lights of the eggs. Then all the eggs, every last entire single one of them, transform into puffs of faintly glowing mist. Moments after that, the mist disappears into thin air, and the ocean is pure black once more, and calm, and eggless.

Me and Shoelace hold one another and stare at Shade Girl, whose eggs are also transforming, turning into mist before our eyes. The mist is wispy. Golden-coloured.

Then, like the eggs in the sea, Shade Girl is gone.

Her egg-sac body is gone. All that remains of her is a cloud of shimmering fog. A cloud that weaves itself into the shape of a grown-up . . .

I gawp at the ghostly golden person suddenly standing at the bottom of the steps. I think I can make out a face. A woman's face? I can't be sure, I can't be certain, but I think so. But, whatever the answer, something about them reminds me of Mum . . . something about their presence I can't put into words, yet which feels like safety . . .

The ghostly person blinks. Unlike Mum's curtly cut curls, their hair is long and plaited, and their eyes are sad. Even though their features are hard to make out, I can tell that, if they were solid – if they weren't made from mist and light but flesh and blood – they would be beautiful. They would be absolutely entirely beautiful.

They wear what I think is a flowing gown, like something a prince or a princess would have. On their head rests a tiara, or a thin crown or something. Again, it's hard to know for certain, what with how ghostly they look.

They stare at their shining, trembling hands. They look astonished.

Then the maybe-a-prince or maybe-a-princess peers up the stairs at me and Shoelace, smiles a peaceful smile and shuts their eyes as though in sheer utter absolute relief.

And then they vanish into nothing.

The stench is gone. The heat starts to fade. The sky isn't red any more, but back to its shining patchwork self, and both Shade Girl and the eggs in the ocean are gone—

gone

gone

gone

gone

gone.

But, when me and Shoelace turn to the doorframe, the way back home is still gone, too.

Artwork to come

Where I discover that,

with my hand in yours,

I'm happy

CHAPTER 0

It's so much. It's sooo, so much.

And, for a moment, I don't worry about the door, but let myself collapse on my back and stare straight upwards at the million billion stars in the treasure-chest sky. Up there, there is a colour, I think, for every single feeling that explodes in my miracle body.

Is it possible to feel every emotion at the precise same second? It can't be. They'd cancel each other out! Yet happiness swells in my belly while tidal waves of exhaustion thunder through my muscles – if I was in Voxminer, it would be like losing all my health hearts. My breath goes heavy. My legs go weak. My arms weigh the same as mountains, plus my vision swirls and my head pounds, and I want to cry and I want to laugh, and I want to fall asleep forever and ever with my arms round Shoelace.

We did it.

We beat Shade Girl.

I want to dance. I want to go home and flop on the sofa and sob into Mum's lap. How is it literally possible to feel SO MANY THINGS at the same exact time?!

Shoelace wraps her fingers round mine.

. . . I'm nearly twelve, and twelve's almost a teenager – and I guess there's something about being a teenager, something reeeally big, which I've never thought much about before. But I'm sure as Voxminer thinking about it now. Because being a teenager's meant to be when girls and boys start hanging out, and holding hands and stuff, and going on dates.

Except, after tonight, I like Shoelace's hand. I like how it feels: I like how soft it is in mine. And, even though I'm almost nearly an almost-a-teenager, suddenly I don't know how I feel about holding hands that don't belong to Shoelace.

Maybe I don't want to hold anyone else's hand.

Shoelace jerks me from my thoughts. 'Roars?' she whispers.

I twist my head to look at her. She's on her back, too, wheezing yet smiling.

My cheeks flush. Why is it hard to talk all of a sudden?!

'Y-yeah?'

'Um, I've been thinking,' she says, 'and . . . let's take a break from Voxminer, yeah? I'll come to yours every night, and we can do other stuff together instead. You'll come to mine, too. Deal?'

She says 'deal' super firmly, like she's not actually asking a question but just explaining how things are going to be from now on.

But then she swallows. She grips my hand harder like she's trying to say something else – and the weird, delicious cold from earlier floods back into my belly in an instant, that cold feeling in my stomach like I'd never felt before. This time, however, it happens as I'm peering into Shoelace's eyes, and the feeling's stronger than ever, and I hope it never, ever stops.

A smile breaks out across my face. 'Let's not go swimming for a bit either,' I add. 'I'm sick of it. I think I broke some kind of swimming record tonight.'

We giggle, and, for a second, everything feels normal enough that it's only when my breath catches that we notice how cold it's become.

A breeze picks up over the ocean; it's as freezing as being dumped in an iceberg biome with only your dressing gown on. My teeth chatter, my breath mists, and I wrap my arms round my chest. My arms and legs are still bare, and all I've got to keep me warm is my still-damp swimming costume.

Shoelace gasps and points at the sky. 'Roars! Look!'

But I've noticed it, too.

It's snowing.

There aren't any clouds, yet somehow it's actually snowing. The snowflakes drift straight from the stars, blown around by the ice-cold wind. They're not normal snowflakes either, but glow a soft pale white. Soon it's tricky to tell where the snowflakes end and the stars and the glimmerings of nebula begin.

'D'you reckon it's this c-cold here all the time?' Shoelace says, still gawping at the glowing snowflakes.

We sit up properly. The blue-grey floor gets colder, colder and colder.

I shrug. 'I g-guess so? Shade Girl must've been using magic to make it warmer. For her eggs. Or s-something.'

I feel I should say more, but my thoughts wobble about as though slipping on ice. Now the relief of surviving Shade Girl is fading, all I can think about is Shoelace's hand, and the empty doorframe, and the fact that there's no way home for us.

And the water is rising again.

The bottom steps have flooded. It's so chilly that shards of ice form against the staircase.

I can't think straight. I can't think. I just need to be close as I can to Shoelace.

The snow falls harder. My damp skin is so frosty that it tingles.

But I scowl because I went through waaaay too much tonight just for me and Shoelace to freeze to death on some random stairs in the middle of the sea. No, I'm going to get us back home, and I'm going to see Mum, and I don't even care if she knows I broke all ten of her ground rules. I'm going to hug her. I'm never going to let go of her in my whole entire life.

Me and Shoelace are NOT going to die here!

I get to my feet. I pull Shoelace up and study the empty doorframe.

'R-Roars?'

I feel the doorframe with my fingertips. 'There's got to be a way out,' I mutter back. 'We have magic here. Ben said so. Remember?'

Shoelace's eyes brighten. 'You saying we can bring it back? The door? You reckon we can make it lead to my room again?'

The water keeps on rising. The staircase is almost gone.

But I nod, and we don't say anything else, just place our palms against the frame.

I don't know how to do this; I've got nooo idea how the tug-on-my-heart actually worked earlier. If I did it before, though, then by Riley's Sword of Sorrows and Detective Mermaid's submersible magnifying glass, by the claws of Monster Kitten Fighting Force, by every last Voxfriend in Voxminer, I can do it again.

Shoelace thinks of her home, her room, her parents. She doesn't need to say any of this out loud, but I know her so well that I can feel it.

I think of Mum.

I think of her warmth. I remember the smell of her freshly washed work things when she uses too much washing powder. I imagine the taste of her home-made chips, then picture her tucking me into bed and reading the latest Shimmer Squad novel to me.

I miss Mum reading me Shimmer Squad novels. She says I'm getting too old for stuff like that. But when I see her again I'm going to beg her to read them to me.

Or maybe I won't beg her to read me a book in bed, but we can do something else that almost-nearly-twelve-year-olds do with their parents, like go out for burgers, or watch a funny Christmas film whilst snugly wrapped in our warmest thickest dressing gowns. I guess it doesn't matter what. Just so long as, whatever we do, we do it together.

'Oh my gosh! Roars!'

The light appears so suddenly that I gasp. There's no flash of magic or anything, no blast of noise like in films. Instead, the doorframe just fills with pure silver light, and the light washes over us and makes everything brighter.

I smile at the light. It's different from before, and not just because it's soft silver instead of gold.

I feel the difference. I actually for real feel it.

Even to myself, the feeling's hard to explain, but it's not bad or anything: in fact, from the tingle in my heart, I can tell for certain that this isn't some last-second trick of Shade Girl's or anything weird like that. It's just . . . different. Different in a way I can't put a finger on, except that my bones buzz with warm excitement, and the song of adventure suddenly carols in the deep of my soul.

I don't know where the doorway leads any more.

I think Shoelace feels the adventure song, too, because she cocks her head and says, 'This . . . still goes back to my room, don't it? Is this how it looked before? The first time you were here?'

I don't know how to answer. Apart from being silver, the light in the doorway does look the same as before. But that song in my heart . . . that tingle in my bones . . .

Shoelace speaks in a whisper.

An excited whisper.

'If it don't go to my room, where d'you reckon it goes?'

I don't answer. If we walk through the light, I don't know where we'll end up, except that sheer, sheer instinct tells me that it won't be Shoelace's bedroom. It could be anywhere. Anywhere.

Shining snowflakes fall, the wind whips at us, and the ocean's risen so much that icy water splashes over my toes. Another minute more and our feet will be totally covered.

Perhaps the light goes to my bedroom instead, and that's why it's a different colour? Or perhaps it goes to school? Or to me and Shoelace's local swimming pool or somewhere even wilder? Perhaps we'll end up inside Voxminer, in Kittentopia! Or in the stars, surrounded by herds of zoxens grazing off fresh moonlight!

A grin tugs at my mouth.

Until we walk through, there's just no way of knowing. No way at all . . .

Shoelace takes my hand; a grin of her own crosses her face, and my heart flutters. Then she looks me right in the eye, nods and says,

'Let's do it together.'

I nod and smile back at her. 'Yeah,' I whisper. 'Together . . .'

And, before we can change our minds, we face the light, face our future and step on through. Because no matter what waits on the other side – good or bad, scary or wonderful – as long as I'm with Shoelace, I can face it. We can face it. As long as we're together, there's nothing in the whole entire universe we can't do.

As long as we're together, it means one thing and one thing only.

It means we're *safe*.